"What's wrong with me?"

Carolina didn't understand Will's question. "What?"

"I have to know why you won't let me get close."

"I'm thirty-six, and I'm flattered that you—

"I don't give a damn how old you are!"

She took one small step away from him. "You're too young for me, and you're not the type of man I want to get involved with. I've gone through a divorce and if you're trying to make me feel better about it, I—"

The look on her face hit him like a blow. She didn't want him. She'd confessed to needing a man, but she wasn't interested in him. Who then? Her ex-husband?

Drawing in a long breath, Will decided to try one more tack. He wasn't sure he could force the words out of his mouth, they hurt so much. "Carolina, in the dark, I can be anyone you want me to be..."

As usual, to the A-Team:
Anne and Ann—for their help and their abuse.

Thanks to:
Mike Goldberg, timber framer extraordinaire and excellent
boat driver—even though he thought the story line would
be more fun as a murder mystery.

Judie Raiford, wild woman of Roswell and designer of
unique jewellery—for her enthusiasm, for the details of her
work, and for Mike.

Finally, to Laura Shin, my editor. Thanks for liking what I
do. I'll miss you.

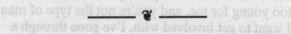

LYN ELLIS
is also the author
of this novel in
Temptation

DEAR JOHN...

IN PRAISE OF YOUNGER MEN

BY

LYN ELLIS

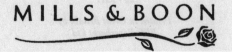

MILLS & BOON

*MILLS & BOON and the Rose Device are trademarks of the publisher.
TEMPTATION is a trademark of Harlequin Enterprises II B.V., used
under licence.
First published in Great Britain in 1995
by Harlequin Mills & Boon Limited, Eton House, 18-24 Paradise Road,
Richmond, Surrey TW9 1SR*

© Gin Ellis 1995

ISBN 0 263 79493 8

21 - 9511

*Printed in Great Britain by
BPC Paperbacks Ltd*

By the time he stood before her at the bottom of the
porch steps, she'd decided he would have even fit
through the door of her former studio and bedroom,
much less find any room in the narrow single bed.

1

As Carolina stared at her newest employee and un-
solicited future housemate, the first word that came to
mind was big. With a sinking feeling, she saw him push
the truck door closed and saunter toward her, seeming
to grow taller with every step. He walked with an easy,
totally male grace, in a body comfortable with its size
and sure of its physical strength and balance. The body
of a man who knew and accepted the fact that he would
never be able to enter a room unnoticed.

What had her brother Brad gotten her into this time?
Why had she let him send her the portfolio? Why had
she fallen in love with one particular house plan? A plan
that involved a heavy timber construction, that required this friend of her brother's, Will Case, to build.

"What do you mean, he can live *here?*" She'd been
incredulous at her younger brother's suggestion. The
thought of cleaning up in the wake of one of Brad's fra-
ternity brothers after he had trashed the kitchen or—
she grimaced—the bathroom was going to take more
than her brother's considerable charm to dispel.

"Look," she'd sighed into the phone, "I hired this guy
on your recommendation and on the strength of his
portfolio. Living with him wasn't part of the deal."

But she'd found out it *was* part of the deal. Written
into the contract, signed and sealed. He required on-site
lodging, and the only place within twenty miles was her
small cabin.

By the time he stood before her at the bottom of the porch steps, she'd decided he would never even fit through the door of her former studio and bedroom, much less find any comfort in the narrow single bed she'd scrounged from her friend Sue Ann. She'd also decided that this man, besides being the same age, was nothing like her playful, normal-size, sports-addicted brother. And for some reason Carolina, despite knowing she was older and the boss, suddenly felt at an unequivocal disadvantage.

He removed the heavily tinted sunglasses he was wearing and slid them into the upper pocket of his denim work shirt before extending one sizable hand. "Will Case," he said.

The low, sure timbre of his voice settled around her as Carolina stared into eyes that mirrored the fresh green of the surrounding pines. Pretty eyes, she conceded, even with the tiny squint marks at the corners. Sort of wasted on a man—a tall man, at that. Her eye-to-eye view was made possible by the fact that she was standing on the porch steps.

His hand was warm and slightly rough. It enveloped hers only long enough to be polite. "Carolina Villada," she replied before his fingers slipped away from hers.

He looked over his shoulder and gave a short whistle. Her brother's reassurances began to stretch and fray. *He's one of the best at what he does,* Brad had said. *All he seems to need are his tools and a place to sleep.*

And his dog, Carolina added silently with dismay, as she watched the gangly weimaraner race toward her. Like an overzealous masher, the dog bounded up the stairs of the porch, nearly knocked her on her behind, then slobbered greetings all over her hands and arms as she tried to push him down.

"Fang, come!"

Fang? The dog danced away and followed Will in the direction of his battered blue pickup truck. Fighting a frown, Carolina dusted the sandy paw prints off the denim covering her thighs, then watched as Will pulled out something red and raggedy from the bed of the truck. With a negligent flick of his arm, he sent the object flying end-over-end into the surrounding woods.

"Go play, boy." The low-voiced command conveyed more amused affection than discipline. The dog took off like a gray-furred, heat-seeking missile.

By the time Will made his way to the porch steps, the dog reappeared, shaking the red treasure he'd retrieved from the woods with a body-engaged vengeance. Will bent down to thump the dog's ribs companionably.

"This is Fang." He twisted the red object out of Fang's mouth and the dog sat up, quivering, poised for the next throw, completely ignoring Carolina and his introduction.

Carolina experienced another, less subtle pang of alarm. The hard-won peace and order of her life seemed to be crumbling around her. "Nobody mentioned a dog."

Will's eyes cut to her at the same instant he tossed the toy into the woods once more. His expression balanced between annoyance and caution. "You don't like dogs?"

Carolina crossed her arms as the dog dashed away. Of course she liked dogs. But in a move more typical of her brother, Will had shown up with one without asking her opinion or permission. She wondered if Brad had known and neglected to tell her.

"Dogs are fine, but not in the cabin," she said after a moment, answering his question with a condition. "He'll have to stay outside." Best to set the ground rules now while she was standing between the two of them and the door. A dog Fang's size in a place as small as her cabin was a forecast for disaster.

On his return, Fang dropped the red toy at Will's well-worn work boots. Will squatted and slung one arm over Fang's back in an almost protective stance. The dog's tongue lolled over his teeth in a canine imitation of a harmless grin.

"He's no trouble."

But he won't be any trouble. Brad, her macho, twenty-nine-year-old, 'little' brother had been talking about his best buddy Will, but he'd sounded the same when he was ten and had brought home a stray puppy. Carolina almost smiled.

Unfortunately, she'd had to clean up that puppy's mess, too.

Carolina rested both hands on her hips in her best challenging, big-sister stance. She looked directly into Will's forest green eyes and said, "That's what I heard about you."

Instead of trying to defend himself or convince her of his amiability, Will smiled. A dangerous, flagrant, playful smile that seemed to fit the precise definition of trouble. A smile that lasered across ten feet of empty air, directly through Carolina's clothes to her skin, elevating the usually sedate rhythm of her pulse to a pounding in her throat.

Something inside her opened and warmed. She couldn't look away, and that surprised her more than if she'd been struck by a bolt of lightning on a cloud-less day—and enjoyed it, for God's sake.

With a shrug of his wide shoulders, Will's smile faded to an amused twist of his lips. "That depends on who you ask, and what kind of trouble," he said. He patted the dog and straightened to his full height. "Fang will be fine outside." He eyed the cabin critically. "He needs a lot of room, and this place looks pretty small."

Torn by the need for a time-out to sit and calm down, yet stung by his subtle criticism of her cabin, Carolina took in a slow breath. She reminded herself that she was in charge here. "That's what I told Brad." She lifted one hand toward the front door. "I don't understand this on-site lodging stipulation. Now that you've seen the place, surely you agree you'd be more comfortable in a motel in town."

"Not likely," Will said as he propped one foot on the second step and rested a hand on his thigh. His gaze roamed over her face, long enough to make Carolina want to fidget. His fingers shifted against the denim of his jeans. "I'd spend most of my time running back and forth.

"Timber work is hard, but when you have a feel for it, it's like a dance. Contracting the entire house is much more complicated. Instead of dancing, I'll be directing the music, and I won't have the time or the energy to commute."

When Carolina didn't comment, he continued, "Besides, Brad says you're a good cook."

"Brad would talk your dog out of his Alpo rather than fix something for himself."

"Well—" the trace of a smile haunted his lips "—I'm willing to take my turn, but it would probably be best if I leave the cooking to you. I nearly blew up the chemistry lab when I was in college."

"Great," Carolina replied, hoping the sinking sensation in her stomach wasn't a premonition. "What were you making?"

"Homemade smoke bombs."

Carolina stared at the mischievous glint in his green eyes and found it easy to picture him as a juvenile delinquent. "I hope you've outgrown those kinds of hobbies," she said with a liberal amount of warning in her voice. That's all she needed—to be trapped in the same house with a practical joker.

"Some of them," he admitted with a smirk. "The rest I just got better at."

An inner smile tugged at her, but Carolina fought it. Time to get serious.

"Listen," she began. "I design and make jewelry for a living. I have not one, but three big shows this summer, and I need my private time to work. In order for this living arrangement to succeed, you're going to have to respect my privacy. In a cabin this size—"

Will's smirk disappeared. "I'll stay out of your way," he said. "I need a bed, a bathroom and a meal once in a while. I don't expect you to keep me company." The provoking slant of his lips returned. "Unless, of course, you can't resist...."

"Believe me," Carolina said slowly and distinctly, intending to cut short any ideas he might have in that direction, "I *can* resist." She turned toward the front door of the cabin. "Get your stuff and come on in. We'll have to see if you can even fit in the extra room I have."

2

WILL STOMPED his boots on the welcome mat and followed Carolina through the front door of her cabin. He set down his tool pouch near the wall inside the entrance and adjusted the strap of the duffel bag over his shoulder.

The cabin was small and clean and well built, even though he recognized the round-log design of a prefab kit. It was also, in his opinion, filled with too much furniture and overflowing with...art. The room looked like a cross between an enticing antique shop and a funky museum.

A leaning stack of books stood in the corner begging for a bookcase; two colorful Navaho blankets were draped over the couch, another over a leather chair; several desert landscapes decorated the small amount of wall space between the doorframes. Rocks and pieces of petrified wood or cactus were arranged across the mantel among elaborate metal candle holders, while the fireplace was flanked by twin piles of split logs. Every end table held a lamp or a piece of art, every window ledge was crowded with plants. Any available gap seemed to be filled. A true collector would have waded in with a smile. A claustrophobic would have thrown himself screaming from the first open window.

Will liked neatness, space. This place was neat in a jammed sort of way, but there were definitely no empty spaces.

Resigned, he drew in a deep breath and immediately forgot about the lack of room. An enticing aroma filled his nostrils.

"What are you cooking?"

Carolina had reached the narrow steps leading to the second level when his question stopped her. She turned and absently waved a hand toward the small kitchen area off a short hallway to the right. "I'm baking a chicken...for chicken and rice. I hope you're not a vegetarian." She threw him a challenging look.

"I'm a foodatarian," he said, hiking his duffel higher to wend his way between the furniture toward her. "And if it tastes as good as it smells," he promised, "I'll be happy with a corner to sleep in and a clear path to the kitchen."

As he followed Brad's sister up the narrow flight of stairs, certain things about her began to come into sharper focus. Like the fact that she had a great ass. Brad had neglected to mention that pertinent fact when he'd coerced Will into giving his word to be on his best behavior. His best buddy had also failed to mention honey-colored eyes and the rhythmic sway of the braid confining her long chestnut hair as she walked. When Brad had talked him into building this house for his older sister, he'd expected *old*. Wrong. Carolina was a seriously good-looking woman. Well, he sighed inwardly, he'd promised to build her a house.

That ought to keep him busy enough, and tired enough...although after a good tiring day's work there was nothing he liked better than—

"Here it is," Carolina said, turning to face her new housemate. In the tight confines of her upstairs hallway, she was having some difficulty catching her breath. Will was easily the largest man she'd ever been in close contact with. And they *were* close. He and his duffel bag seemed to fill the entire space; a foot taller than she and with shoulders wide enough to block the horizon, he loomed over her. Her hard-earned common sense told her she ought to be afraid. She could feel his expectant gaze, smell the male scents of after-shave and sun-warmed skin. But there was no fear . . . there was something more like anticipation. What was wrong with her? This man was one of her brother's buddies. Good lord, she was a half dozen years older than he was.

And Paul was twelve years older than the younger woman he'd abandoned their marriage for, her traitorous mind taunted.

Startled by unwanted thoughts of her ex-husband, Carolina took a sudden step backward, farther away from Will. "Uh, this is where Brad sleeps when he visits. It used to be my studio."

Will stared through the doorway without expression.

Seeing for the first time how the tiny room must look from his large perspective, Carolina nervously moved through the low doorway. Earlier, she'd piled several cardboard boxes along one side of the room to get them out of the way. Now she realized she'd have to move them somewhere else.

She bent to pick up the closest one and backed up, intending to turn around. "I'm sorry. I haven't unpacked some of these boxes since the divorce. I'll move them downstairs so that—" She was brought up short by the warm, solid wall of a male body against her backside. Mortified by the intimate contact, Carolina froze.

Will had better reflexes. He quickly stepped away. She heard a thump and a low curse. Then his duffel bag was shoved past her to land with a bounce on the bed. Guiltily, she turned to find him with his neck bent forward, eyes shut, rubbing one hand over the back of his head. His jaw looked tight.

"Are you okay? I'm sorry. I—"

"I'm fine." He spoke through gritted teeth. "I hit my head on the doorframe. Was this cabin built for midgets?"

Carolina stacked the box she held in her hands on top of the others, grasped the solid weight of Will's arm and urged him toward the bed. They had to turn in a slow do-si-do in order to reach it. "Sit down. Let me look."

"It's all right," he grouched. But when his fingers came away from his hair, they were smeared with blood. "Damn."

Will didn't want her fussing over him. As a matter of fact, if she would just leave this closet of a room he knew he would feel better immediately. He wouldn't have hit his head in the first place if she hadn't backed into him butt first.

"Let me get some cotton and alcohol."

Fine, Will thought as he listened to her rapid footsteps thump on the stairs. He glared at the top of the nonregulation doorframe with murderous intentions only a carpenter would dream of. Maybe he'd use a chain saw.

When Carolina returned with her first-aid supplies, she seemed to hesitate at the door before coming toward him. She probably thought he was angry at her instead of the solid wood he'd tried to dent with his head. He knew he should smile and put her at ease, but his head hurt and he didn't want her touching him.

When she moved to stand between his knees, he had to lower his gaze to the floor or he would have been staring at her breasts—at extremely close range. With another woman as attractive as this one, he might have taken advantage of the opportunity to at least look. But this was Brad's sister, Brad's *older* sister, although that distinction was lost on him. Guessing the ages of women had never been one of his priorities. And, no matter what Carolina's age might be, she looked good—Will drew in a breath—and she smelled great. How in the hell was he going to get through several months of sharing this small and stuffed cabin with her? Bumping into each other every time they turned around? He studied the laces of her Reeboks as her fingers pushed into his hair and decided he was going to kill his good buddy Brad.

With the detached mercy of a Mother Teresa, Carolina blotted the cut with a cotton ball. After one cooling stroke, his scalp seemed to catch fire. Will sucked in a quick lungful of air, then pulled away.

"Are you a sadist, or what?"

One of her hands tightened on his shoulder and pulled him close again. "It's only alcohol. It's a small scrape but you don't want it to get infected."

She was clucking over him like a mother with her five-year-old, and he didn't appreciate it. He certainly didn't feel like a five-year-old, not with her breasts practically pressed into his face. He felt cornered. Well, if she couldn't reach his head, she'd leave him alone. His hands captured her arms above the elbows. He firmly set her away from him, then stood up. "It'll be fine, thanks."

He expected her to put a little distance between them when he released her, but she held her ground. She looked up at him with a slight frown. "You sure?"

For an instant, as he stared into her light brown eyes, he wasn't sure of anything. Except that she truly was concerned about his head. It surprised him—the concern. Most women had other reasons for wanting to get close to him, for wanting to touch . . .

"Yeah, I'm sure." His voice sounded gruff to his own ears. He brought one hand up and rubbed his thumb along the dried smudge of blood on his fingers. "Where can I wash my hands?"

In a flurry of motion, she became businesslike again. She picked up the alcohol and screwed on the top. "The bathroom is downstairs. Follow me." As she stepped through the door, she glanced toward the low-hanging doorframe, and her eyes met his, conveying either apology or warning. But she didn't say anything.

His lips twisted with grim humor. Smart woman.

AFTER WASHING his hands, Will found Carolina in the kitchen. She was bending over, peering into the open oven. He couldn't forestall the rush of pure admiration that ran though him. She definitely had a great—

She jumped suddenly, as if she'd been pinched, and faced him with one hand pressed over her heart. "Rule number one. Don't sneak up on me like that," she said, breathless. Before he could defend himself, she gave a short laugh and peeled the oven mitt off her hand. "I'm not used to having someone else around."

Why did he feel the need to apologize? He hadn't been sneaking, but he had been admiring the fit of her jeans. The way her braided hair cascaded over her shoulder to rest on the swell of her breast. He bit down on the word *sorry* and changed the subject. "I'd like to walk over to the site before it gets dark," he said. "If you're busy, point me in the right direction. I can find it on my own."

She dropped the mitt on the countertop and rubbed her hands down her thighs. Will fought to keep his gaze level. "I'll show you. The chicken needs a few more minutes in the oven."

The sun was low in the sky by the time they left the cabin. Fang raced around them in ever-widening circles as Will followed Carolina down the path to the site for the new house. She pointed out the newer, secondary building behind the cabin and explained that it housed her jewelry studio. She offered to give him a tour at another time if he was interested.

"Watch your step," she said, then used a strategically placed boulder to cross over a small gully that cut through the rocky ground.

Will looked around with interest. He'd been through the southern part of Arizona once, years before, and until he saw the city of Prescott and the surrounding area with his own eyes, he would never have guessed northern Arizona could be so different. Certainly not as green as Washington, but without the harsh terrain of the Sonoran Desert. Higher in altitude, this part of the state was a cooler plateau with forests of scrub oak, ponderosa pine and juniper on hills broken by intermittent stacks of granite boulders, like the backbone of the earth, protecting the green valleys between.

Stakes with fluttering plastic tape and string stretched into a square marked the building site. Carolina had chosen the ideal place to build. The land sloped gently downward and overlooked a huge formation of rock. The only trees that had been cut were the ones that would directly interfere with the house itself or the road coming in. Otherwise, the woods surrounding the site were intact. It would be easy to imagine his house here.

His house? Her house, he amended. He would find another perfect setting to build his house. Someday.

"What do you think?" Carolina asked.

He wasn't sure if she was making conversation or if his opinion mattered. He turned a slow circle before answering. "It's great. I can see why you chose this spot."

"I love it here." She focused on a distant point across the valley and drew in a breath. The waning rays of the sun brightened the side of her hair, touching each dark strand with gold. "I've tramped over nearly every acre of my land, but this is the place I always come back to."

Her certainty touched something in Will. He couldn't remember any place he'd been back to once the job was done, once he'd moved on. He wondered why, then pushed the question away. He didn't like to wonder. "Well, that's good, because after we start the foundation, you can't change your mind."

She faced him then, her features serious, her eyes lit with the sun's fire and with her own determination. "I've had ten years to dream about this house, and two years to plan it. I won't change my mind."

No, I guess you won't, Will thought, staring into her gold-dazzled brown eyes. He glanced away, toward the lowering sun. "I'll get everything moving tomorrow, find out exactly when the crew can start the foundation. Did you apply for the permits and contract for water?"

"Yes on the permits. I got two bids for the water, and I waited because the difference in price had to do with the size of pipe, and I wasn't sure which would be best."

"I'll take a look at them. I'm a little rusty at this my-self. I don't usually contract the whole job. I do my timber thing and hit the road."

"Brad talked you into this, didn't he?"

"Well, yes and no." Will propped one boot on the corner stake. Brad was the closest he had come in life to having a brother. Sisters were nice, but brothers were buddies. They understood each other.

Be careful with my sister, he had said to Will. *She's had a tough time, and she's still in love with the guy.*

"I'd do just about anything for Brad," Will began, with an understatement that nearly made him laugh. "I know he'd do the same for me," he continued. "In this case, Brad asked me to help his sister out, but he also knows I need the work. I'll try to save you some money and—"

"I'm not worried about the money. I usually barter for most things I want and haggle over my work for someone else's. But not for this."

Will frowned. She seemed smart. He couldn't be-lieve she would be so foolish as to tell a contractor that the price didn't matter. Even one who was her broth-er's best friend. "Somebody needs to worry about money," he warned. "You're already building more house than you'll ever need. If I were you, I'd cut down the plan and—"

She crossed her arms, ready to do battle. "You're not me. So how could you know what I need? I'm not one of those starving artists people find so romantic. I want the house I picked out, without cutting corners. And I can afford it—in real dollars."

"All right." He'd stepped into it now. He'd stubbed his size-eleven boot on an independent woman's inde-pendence. He raised his hands in surrender then jammed them into the back pockets of his jeans. Brad had called his sister "fragile." She didn't seem so at the moment. "Are you having a bad week? Or is it me?"

She looked surprised. "What do you mean?"

"Well, ever since I got out of my truck you've been acting like I'm the enemy. If you don't want me to do the job, say so and I'll leave. No problem." He didn't want to leave, but he wasn't going to spend the next several months working for a woman who didn't like or at least trust him. She might be hurting, but he wasn't the bad guy.

She was silent for a moment. Then she brought up one hand and brushed the wayward strands of hair fluttering at her neck. "It's not really you," she said slowly. "This house is very important...." She paused as if she wasn't sure how much she wished to tell a stranger. "It's special to me. And I won't let anyone change my mind."

Especially a man, Will finished silently. Was he being strung up merely because he was male? He had no doubt that she was serious. If he intended to stay and do this job, he needed to find a little common ground. He tried a different approach—retreat. "Okay. If you tell me what you need, I'll get it done. But I know this house. It's special to me, too. I helped design it. For this arrangement between us to work, you're going to have to trust me. Can you?"

She didn't answer right away, but the guarded look on her face spoke volumes. The sun had fallen below the tree line, and they were left standing in the gathering shadows. Fang's half-muffled barking echoed in the distance.

Without the drama of the afternoon light, Carolina seemed smaller, fragile, just as Brad had said, and Will unaccountably felt like a bully. It was her house, after all, not his. She should be setting him straight on what she wanted. Where had that certainty and independence gone? His gaze drifted from her eyes to the smooth line of her jaw to the strained set of her mouth. Getting over a bad divorce. Was there any other kind? A shaft of anger whipped through him. What had her ex-husband done to make her want to move out into the woods all alone? *It's none of your business, Will,* his self-preservation warned. He backed away from the anger and the question. From experience, he knew he didn't want to know.

He made an attempt to lighten the mood. "You know—" he purposely kept his features solemn "—it could be worse. At least you and I aren't married . . . we're only living together."

After a moment of surprised silence, Carolina laughed.

Then, shaking her head, her features animated by a natural smile, she looked at him as if he'd actually said the right thing. "Okay, timber man. You build my house. And I'll think about trusting you." She extended her hand to seal the bargain.

An unreasonable streak of accomplishment roared through Will. Making a woman laugh was almost as good as making her—well, he shouldn't be thinking about sex where Brad's sister was concerned. His best buddy had made that clear in no uncertain terms. But Will couldn't help grinning. "That's a deal," he said, as his hand closed around hers.

Carolina stared into Will's laughing green eyes, unable to breathe. She could feel her heart expanding, pounding, calling for more oxygen in a hurry. She could hear her head ordering the rest of her body to calm down. But her eyes remained locked with his.

There was nothing extraordinary about Will Case, with the minor exceptions of his clear green eyes and his size. His face had strong lines, but his nose was closer to prominent than classic. His dark blond hair was longish, cut neatly and sun-streaked from working outside, but certainly not the flowing locks of a romantic hero. He was merely a tall, well-built young man with sexy eyes.

Until he smiled.

God. He smiled like a wolf, warm and playful. All full of himself and willing to share. She had hoped her first reaction, when he had smiled at her on the porch, was a fluke. That, since she hadn't been alone with a man for a while, any smile would have touched a nerve, then passed on like the sun striking the angle of a prism.

But it hadn't passed. She was experiencing the same gut-level tremor right this minute, and the shock waves made the rational part of her brain go fuzzy. She had no idea how to fight her response, or even if she wanted to. A pulse of alarm ran through her. She had to fight it. What she wanted from Will had nothing to do with charm and smiles, and everything to do with building her house, her new life.

To retain some semblance of control, she lowered her eyes and pulled her hand away. She shivered and briskly rubbed both hands up and down her upper arms. "It's getting cool," she said, hoping her voice wouldn't fail her. "Let's go back." Unable to look at him again, to gauge whether he had noticed how his smile affected her, she turned toward the trail.

Will followed her along the trail, confused but convinced they were on better terms. He didn't understand how she could be smiling and warm one minute, as cool as granite the next. But then, he had never claimed to understand women. He understood a few things about them, physical things, sexual things and some of the head games they could play. Their moods and minds were a completely different matter.

Fang barked again, even farther away. A distant crashing of bushes gave the only indication of his whereabouts. Will gave a sharp whistle to call him.

"Do you think you should tie him up?" Carolina asked over her shoulder.

"Nah. He won't run away." Will whistled once more for good measure.

By the time they reached the porch of the cabin, it was nearly dark. Fang arrived seconds before them. He bounded up the steps spinning and jumping like he'd been waiting hours for their return. Carolina avoided getting tangled in his gyrations but stopped before she reached the door. She took a step backward and bent down. "What's this?"

Something was lying on the mat.

Will squatted next to her and picked up the object. He held it so Carolina could see that it was a dish towel. The towel was wet, and crushed, and dirty, and smelled like dog slobber. But it still had a plastic clothespin clinging to one corner.

"Where's your nearest neighbor?" Will asked innocently.

"About a quarter of a mile down the road," Carolina answered with a sigh.

"Do they have a sense of humor?"

Carolina gave Fang one dark, contemplative look, then she rolled her gaze heavenward in what appeared to be a silent plea for help. She gingerly pulled the towel out of Will's hand. "Let's hope so," she answered as she reached for the doorknob.

DINNER WAS AWKWARD.

Carolina felt as though she'd been assigned to entertain one of the three bears and had been unlucky enough to end up with the extra-large one. She had to admit there was nothing wrong with Will's manners or his appetite. The problem was that each time he entered a room, she realized once again how small and crowded her cabin had become over the past two years. Whenever his gaze followed her, she wondered how she would ever get used to his presence. But worst of all, every time she met his eyes, she remembered her body's reaction to his smile. Trouble.

During dinner, she kept her gaze on her plate or on his hands. His fingers were long and blunt, the nails clipped short. One of the knuckles on his left hand was skinned. He handled the silverware with an economy of movement like he would probably handle a hammer or a pry bar. Carolina felt like screaming—reduced to the contemplation of silverware etiquette.

Had it been so long since she'd entertained a man with dinner conversation? She tried to think back, but only came up with the few times she'd invited some of her friends, with their husbands, over for dinner or drinks. It had been a long time since Paul. Over two years since she'd had to juggle the job of being a socially correct wife. With an inner sigh of frustration, she realized she really had lost touch with the art of small talk.

Nowadays, she usually saved her socializing for gallery openings and shows where she was required to talk about her work or someone else's. Brad's conversation invariably revolved around two topics, sports and women, with an occasional dash of politics thrown in. She searched her mind for something to say that might have relevance to a guy Will's age.

Will checked out Carolina across the table. She didn't respond to his gaze so he centered his attention on the double windows and the dark woods beyond. She'd barely said a word during dinner and he didn't want to push.

He was used to eating with strangers. She, obviously, wasn't. He wondered just how long it had been since she'd been out for dinner, or in this case *in* for dinner with a man. A purely male part of him hoped it had been a long time. As soon as the thought entered his head, his mind countered with, *This isn't a date.* If she wanted silent meals, he'd handle it. But he couldn't get comfortable with the idea that she might be afraid of him. Intimidation wasn't his style. Yet she watched him warily, as if he was some kind of alien who had dropped out of the sky and straight into a chair at her dining room table.

For about three heartbeats he missed the chaos of his sister's house in California where he'd spent the last four months. A house with three annoying but almost human kids under twelve; two rambunctious dogs, one of which belonged to him; one terrorized cat; and finally, his long-suffering, lawyer brother-in-law. Will lifted another forkful of Carolina's chicken and rice into his mouth and the nostalgia faded. His sister, Jeanne, couldn't cook worth a damn. Carolina, on the other hand . . .

"This is really good," he said, hoping to break the tense silence.

"I'm glad you're enjoying it," she answered cautiously.

She seemed to be fascinated by his hands or by the way he used his knife and fork. It reminded him of being watched by the teacher in third grade. He studied the curve of Carolina's lips and wished he could coax one more natural smile to her mouth. Maybe then she would realize he wasn't going to attack her with the silverware.

"You have to tell me what you like—" Carolina stammered to a halt and finally looked at him. He watched in amazement as her face turned an appealing shade of pink.

His lips twitched with the urge to tease her.

"Actually, I'm pretty easy to please . . ." he began.

"Foodwise," she continued quickly, then drew in a breath. The look she gave him could not be mistaken. It spelled warning with a capital W. "I guess what you don't like is more important."

The unpleasant vision of fried liver and onions, one of the few things he wouldn't eat, crossed his mind. She couldn't be that cruel, he decided.

Living in unfamiliar surroundings for months at a time had taught Will one of life's priorities—finding good food and plenty of it. If this meal was any indication, he'd stumbled into Nirvana. He wasn't going to muck it up. Liver or not.

He picked up his napkin, wiped his mouth, then dropped the napkin to the table and smiled a harmless, let's-be-friends smile. "Basically, if you cook it, I'll eat it. And, if everything is as good as this chicken, you may have to call the sheriff to drag me out of here when the job is finished."

She didn't laugh as he had hoped. The blush faded and Carolina gave him one of those tolerant, straight-lipped smiles that his own sister was so good at before she pushed to her feet and picked up her half-empty plate.

"I don't cook breakfast, and I don't eat lunch, but I'll make sure there's plenty of food for you. Feel free to help yourself."

Will watched her disappear into the kitchen, heard the clank of dishes, then running water. He shook his head in bewilderment. Maybe he was trying too hard to be friendly. It seemed like every time he smiled at her, the conversation got frosty. He carefully placed his knife and fork across the empty plate in front of him and wiped his fingers one last time on his napkin.

If he lost ground each time he smiled over the next few months, he might need to call the sheriff to come and *rescue* him.

Carolina stared at the bubbles forming as the sink filled with water. Did other women begin having hot flashes at thirty-six? She'd never admit she had blushed. And she refused to believe that she could sit across from a man, any man, with the possible exception of Daniel Day-Lewis, and not be able to look him in the eye. *This is ridiculous*, she fumed as she fought the infantile urge to stamp her foot.

She shut the water off and pushed back a few strands of hair that had escaped from her braid. She had to calm down. What was happening to her? Why was she worried about what Will Case might think? The very idea infuriated her. He was probably about as sensitive and interesting to talk to as her brother. That meant they had about twenty minutes of solid conversation before they ran completely out of topics.

Carolina washed and rinsed her plate, then jammed it into the dish drainer. She braced her arms on the sink and closed her eyes. Maybe she was having a nervous breakdown. Maybe she'd been alone too—

"Are you feeling all right?" The low rumble of Will's voice sounded concerned and close.

Carolina jumped backward and nearly knocked his plate out of his hands.

"I'm sorry," he apologized quickly, but he didn't seem too sorry. "I wasn't sneaking up on you. I . . ."

Warmth flooded her cheeks again. She took the plate out of his grip. To hell with being careful, she decided. She would treat him the same as Brad. Brad wouldn't be caught dead doing dishes. "Out of my kitchen unless you intend to wash or dry," she ordered in her best big-sister voice.

Will just stood there. "I'll dry."

It was nearly more than Carolina could take. "What?"

He picked up the towel and moved closer to the sink. "I said, I'll dry. It's the least I can do since my cooking could be hazardous to your health—" he glanced around the small kitchen "—and your house."

In Carolina's eyes he seemed to already take up more than half the space allotted to her abbreviated version of a kitchen. She couldn't imagine the two of them working together over the sink without a lot of body contact. Actually, she could imagine it, and that was the problem. The image made her words come out harsher than she intended.

She tried a smile, but it faltered. "No. That's all right. There's not really enough room for both of us."

Will already had one plate in his hand. His lips curved slowly and a smile hovered. "I don't bite . . . well, sometimes I do. But right now, I'm full from dinner so you're safe." He held up the dried plate. "Where does this go?"

"The cabinet on the left, over the stove." Carolina knew when she was being charmed. Now what was up? She moved to the sink and plunged her hands into the water. Will put the plate away and returned to her side.

Carolina gave him a calculating sideways glance. "Are we setting a precedent here? Or are you trying to convince me you're a sensitive guy?"

Will reached across her for the other plate. His chest bumped her shoulder. He dried the plate slowly and watched her for a long unnerving moment. "You guessed it. I'm trying to prove I'm a sensitive guy. Is it working?"

"Look, Will—"

He held up a hand to stop her. Any trace of humor disappeared. "Seriously, I'm trying to make friends. I appreciate your letting me stay here. I know it must be awkward for you. I'm not into scaring women. I don't like the idea that you might be afraid of me."

Carolina's hand stopped in midair. Rivulets of water were running down her arm to her elbow, but she was caught by the concern on Will's face. He really looked worried.

"I'm not afraid of you," she said quickly. "You're Brad's friend and—"

"And you're dripping water all over my boots."

"Oh!" She should have known better than to think he was really being serious and concerned and mature. Before she could stop herself, she reverted to her childhood spats with her brother and hurled the wet sponge she was holding. It hit Will square in the center of his chest with a soggy squish.

"Out!" she ordered.

Even though she was incensed, she had to give him credit, he took the assault gracefully. He held one hand over the wet area as if he'd been shot, but he couldn't seem to stop laughing.

She snatched the plate out of his hand and shoved one solid shoulder. She was beginning to laugh, too. "I said, out."

He raised both hands in surrender. "Wait a minute. I came in here to make peace, not start a war."

Carolina bent to pick up the sponge from the floor. Will backed up a step and extended one hand as if he were facing a loaded gun. "Now . . . be nice. Let's talk this over."

"Being nice has gotten me into trouble more times than I want to think about," she confessed. She braced one hand on her hip, composed herself and gave him what she hoped was a dangerous glare. "I'm not afraid of you."

The wattage of his smile should have blown every fuse in the cabin. "Not afraid is good," he said, then held her gaze for several interminable seconds. Long enough for Carolina to decide she'd pay good money to know what he was thinking at that exact moment. And long enough for her to wish she could look away before she blushed again. "Nice is better," he added.

Carolina let out the breath she'd been holding. "How about tolerant?" When he looked disappointed, she offered, "I'll work on nice."

"Deal."

3

"GOOD MORNING."

Carolina blinked once, then blinked again. Will stood at the bottom of the stairs, wearing jeans with only a towel draped around his neck, and a travel kit balanced in one hand. In the warm, early morning light, he looked like one of those breath-stealing fashion ads—sculpted muscle and well-worn denim. The sight made Carolina's throat go dry. Why didn't he wear baggy, faded T-shirts like her brother?

"Good morning," she managed, and averted her eyes. She wished she'd put on more than her robe over her nightgown, although he didn't seem affected. And why should he be? One of the things she liked about being a thirty-six-year-old divorced woman was not having to be beautiful for a man at seven-thirty in the morning. Besides, he wasn't a man; he was her contractor.

"I made coffee," he announced.

With a self-conscious swipe, she pushed back her hair. "Good," she answered without enthusiasm. She was wondering how she could get past him and into the bathroom without a face-to-face encounter.

"Don't worry, I didn't blow anything up." He smiled at her.

"I'll be down in a minute." She spun on her heels in the direction of her bedroom, stalked through the door and closed it. *I don't believe this!* she fumed as she marched over to the mirror behind her dresser. Her own reflection made her wince. Her hair, which in the past she'd considered one of her best assets, was limp and shifted all to one side. A smudge of mascara darkened the area under one of her eyes. The last straw was a dent running along her cheek like a scar, left by a wrinkle in the pillowcase.

Carolina rubbed her cheek and felt like crying. What difference could it possibly make if Will saw her like this? He wasn't her husband or her lover. He would build her house no matter what she looked like. Why did she care?

Because it had mattered to Paul.

After a long moment of silently arguing the perils and pitfalls of worrying about men and their opinions, Carolina tiredly finger-combed her hair and pulled it into a French braid.

Well, even if Will thought of her as an older sister, she didn't have to walk around looking like a banshee. She efficiently secured the braid, then took a tissue and blotted the smudged mascara. By the time she had finished, she was more awake and composed. She could face anything now—even a twenty-nine-year-old Generation Xer with a pro football player's body.

Standing in front of the full-length mirror on the back of her bedroom door, Carolina pulled the belt of her robe a little tighter and lifted her chin. As she tied the belt in a bow, she heard the sound of footsteps in the hallway. After waiting a moment, she opened the door and made a beeline down the stairs, directly into the safety of the bathroom.

Will had obviously taken a shower and shaved, yet the room was as neat as she would have left it. She flipped on the shower faucets and breathed in the pleasant but nearly forgotten smell of shaving cream and after-shave. Maybe this won't be so bad after all, Carolina thought. If she could get used to sidestepping a large, half-naked man every morning, she might— In the mirror, she saw the reflection of Will's plaid shirt hanging by the hook on the back of the door. With the image came the memory of his bare chest—smooth skin with a fine dusting of hair.

Carolina suddenly felt surrounded. What was wrong with her? Why did he make her so skittish? She'd been around her brother's friends before, plenty of times. Of course she'd never lived with one of them, but nevertheless . . .

After dropping her robe and gown on the counter, Carolina kicked off her panties and stepped into the shower. Will certainly hadn't done anything specific to make her uncomfortable. He hadn't even glanced at her in a familiar, much less lecherous way. No, this physical overreaction was her problem, and she'd have to handle it.

Warm water pummeled her shoulders and back, loosening the grip of her anxiety. The entire situation was actually funny. Her ex-husband would probably find it hysterical that she could mentally make a fool of herself over a younger man. A younger man who probably had droves of women willing to stand in line for his attention. And one who also had absolutely no personal interest in her whatsoever, except for her cooking.

Carolina didn't feel like laughing. If she was to make a list of complications she didn't need in her life right now, wanting a man would be number one. Wanting an attractive, younger man who also happened to be her brother's best friend was like standing on the tracks in a train tunnel and being mesmerized by the bright light closing in from the other end. Emotional suicide.

Paul had taught her to be smarter than that.

She'd get used to Will, she pledged firmly. She had made a deal for the house she loved. The house that would be her sanctuary, that would protect her from ever having her life turned upside down again. If it took her the entire time he was under her roof, she'd get used to him.

When she emerged from the bathroom, Will was waiting. At close range, his upper body, sans towel, filled her vision and stopped her cold. All of Carolina's pledges and protestations fell silent while every nerve ending under her skin seemed to fire at once.

Will didn't appear to notice. "Sorry," he said, shrugging his bare shoulders matter-of-factly. "I forgot my shirt." He ducked around her and reached behind the door.

Pulling the collar of her robe closer over her chest, Carolina practically sprinted for the stairs.

HALF AN HOUR later, they were seated at the dining room table sipping coffee. Will had just eaten three of the best blueberry muffins he'd ever tasted, and in contrast to Carolina's apparent serious mood, he was feeling great and ready to work.

"What's the plan for today?" she asked.

"Today I need a phone and a flat space to do some paperwork."

Carolina set down her cup. "I have a small office in my studio. You can use part of that. Or you can use the portable phone and work here at the table."

Will got to his feet and retrieved the roll of house plans he had brought down earlier. As he spread the paper out on the table in front of her, he said, "I want to show you something. The raw timbers are scheduled to be delivered by flatbed next week. But we've got a lot to do before we need them."

Carolina frowned at the plans.

"This design can be flopped—"

"Just a second." She got up from the table and went into the living room. A moment later she returned with something in her hand. "Don't you dare laugh," she warned as she opened the case and slid on a pair of glasses with round lenses. She sat down and pulled the plans closer as if she intended to ignore his reaction.

Will couldn't let a challenge like that pass. When he didn't speak right away, he got what he wanted. She looked at him, and he had the chance to openly study her face.

He didn't have to lie. He didn't have to be too serious either. "They look good on you. They're very... intellectual looking." Her amber eyes narrowed as if she might be contemplating violence.

"Thank you," she said in a prim voice to match the serious style of her glasses. "Now what did you want to show me?"

All business, no play. Will cleared his throat and started over. He tapped the plans with two fingers. "This design can be built in either direction. Living area to the right or to the left, and so on. I assume you want the front of the house to face the rock formation with the vaulted windows overlooking the valley?" When she didn't answer right away, he added, "That's the way I would build it."

Her expression became guarded. She studied the plans as if they were written in Chinese. "Yes," she answered, tentatively. "Toward the rocks ... but I don't know about this right or left thing. I'm a three-dimensional person. That's why I love making jewelry or working with clay." She poked the blueprint with one finger. "Two-dimensional doesn't compute."

"Come on." Will gestured for her to follow him. As she stood up, she whipped off her glasses and shoved them in the case. He resisted a smile and led her across the living room until they were both standing with their backs to the front door. "Now. When you enter this cabin, your living area is to the left, the kitchen area and back door on the right." She nodded. "Upstairs, you have two bedrooms—left and right—with storage in the middle." As he said it, some wayward part of his mind wondered what Carolina's bedroom was like. Was she sleeping in the other utilitarian twin bed that matched the one in his room? Or was there a larger version, made for two people to sleep together?

Keep your mind on the house, his conscience prodded. "If you plan to have the front of the house with the windows toward the east—I mean the rocks—then you'll enter by the rear door unless you walk up the stairs to the deck." He touched her shoulders lightly and turned her around. "Everything you are used to will be backward."

She propped her hands on her hips and sighed. "I don't know . . ." She pivoted to study the room.

"Just tell me this," he said, moving to stand close behind her. Without warning, the memory of her accidentally backing into him the day before fogged his brain. He checked his forward movement so it wouldn't happen again and brought his mind to the question. He raised his left hand over her shoulder. "Do you want to walk in the door and see your living room off to the left with the vaulted ceiling and windows where the stairs are now? Or do you see it on the right, where the—"

"On the left," she said.

He looked at the top of her head, over the intricate braid of her hair, to the side of her face. His gaze stopped at the smooth bare skin just above the collar of her blouse, on a small birthmark. He couldn't pull his eyes away. The inclination to touch that rose-colored mark with his tongue nearly scalded him. He concentrated on controlling his voice. "You're sure?"

She hesitated a moment, and Will contemplated the unfairness of it all. Why did he have to be attracted to his best friend's sister? Was it merely the fact that they were in close proximity? Maybe, although in the past he'd always been careful about who and when and where he was attracted. He'd perfected the art of the short-term, mutual-pleasure association, but it didn't extend to his clients, especially to Brad's sister. Especially to Brad's *divorced* sister. And, according to Brad, Carolina was still in love with her ex-husband.

Divorced women were treacherous ground for his peace of mind, particularly the ones who couldn't quite get over their ex. He had learned enough from bitter experience to keep his distance from women who were looking for an available male until their ex-husbands came back. There was no way he would forget that lesson.

Carolina was a no-nonsense, successful, good-looking woman. Very difficult to ignore. But, according to Brad, she'd been hurt, and Will had agreed to ignore—

Suddenly she turned and he was riveted by those honey eyes. "Yes, I'm sure," she answered.

Standing close enough to kiss, Will thought, and she didn't bat an eyelash. He might as well be fresh out of grade school for all the effect he seemed to have on her.

That in itself was a novelty. Most women couldn't wait to get closer. He nodded, stepped away from her and started for the dining room. "I'll take care of it."

The seismic shock of her hand on his bare arm stopped him. Awareness seemed to emanate from the contact. He glanced at the fingers balanced on his skin and waited. She pulled her hand away as if she'd trespassed, and gave him an assessing look.

"You said you know this house. What do you think? Left or right?"

He shrugged, suddenly tired of the conversation and irritated by the way she could influence him with a mere touch. He wanted to say, "Don't mess with me, lady. I'm not the kind of guy who plays games." But the sad thing was, he didn't think she *was* messing with him. She didn't want to play games. She wanted to build a house.

"Left," he said, knowing he should be happy that she was asking for his opinion but feeling deflated just the same. "After I saw this cabin, I decided to build the new place with the same basic layout. But I figured I'd better let you choose. It's your house, not mine, and I'm here to build it the way you want."

He hadn't intended to be so curt, but the words had tumbled out that way. She didn't seem offended. Her reaction was swift and direct. She said, "Thank you."

As CAROLINA prepared for bed that night, she concluded that the first full day—of the next two months of her life—with Will Case had been a success. He'd spent most of the day on the phone, checking, arranging and cajoling the local subcontractors and suppliers.

She'd used the morning making space in different parts of the cabin to stow the boxes she'd removed from Will's room.

Will's room. The idea wasn't so strange now. He was a nice young guy trying to do the job she'd hired him for. And he wasn't a slob. Now, if she could only cool down . . .

The afternoon had been a little more difficult. He'd accomplished what he could by telephone and planned to go into town tomorrow. He'd decided to hike around a bit with Fang and get a good look at the rest of the property. Carolina frowned as she pulled her gown over her head. He'd invited her to go along with them, but out of self-preservation, she declined. He'd been here a day and a half, and she already needed time away from him.

She'd used the excuse of working, which was valid because she'd spent the afternoon trying a new design. The hours hadn't been productive, however. The thin copper wire she planned to coax into a graceful spiral seemed determined to break at the stress points. It was a good thing she hadn't been working with gold.

The sight of Will when he returned from his hike, smiling, windblown, smelling of pine trees and fresh air, made Carolina wonder if she had reached her own stress point. Had she been alone too long? She had friends, work, a healthy income, a beautiful new home in the works. She didn't need a man, didn't want one. So why was Will so disruptive to her peace of mind?

Hormones. That's all she could figure.

She climbed into bed, switched out the lamp and stared at the darkened ceiling. Was that what had happened to Paul? Had he woken up one day, looked in the mirror and stumbled into a mid-life crisis? She'd always accused him of feeding his ego by surrounding himself with beautiful young women. Wasn't that the ultimate image for men? Carolina knew that for her, a decision to turn to younger men would be deadly for her already damaged ego. Age was viewed differently by men and women. According to American society, part of being a successful male meant having a beautiful young woman at your side. If a woman with a few wrinkles pursued a younger man, however, she was an object of pity or derision. Paul had been four years older than she, and he'd found it necessary to find someone even younger.

He'd left her. It still hurt after all this time. The surprise—no, the shock had worn off, but the compressed ache of betrayal remained like a blade lodged in her heart. She'd been a good wife. She'd spent ten years being helpful, loving. Putting aside her dreams of a home and family for Paul's career, thinking everything was fine. And then he'd left her because she wasn't twenty something anymore.

She'd never be twenty something again. She'd given those years to Paul.

The darkness around her was so still, her own breathing sounded loud. She sighed and tugged the sheet a little higher. What could she possibly have that would interest someone Will's age? Why should she even worry about it? Will wasn't bent on seducing her, and she certainly didn't intend to seduce him. The very thought made her cringe. He would probably laugh in her face, or worse, feel sorry for her.

But something about those long shut-away emotions made her sad. Was she prepared to live a life without passion? Not the passion of creating beautiful things like her jewelry. But the breathless flight of physical pleasure fueled by sparks between two people.

Between a woman and a man.

Unexpected tears filled her eyes. She'd had her chance at passion with Paul, and that had fallen flat. Was that the end of it? One chance and then— No. She wouldn't think about it. When she was ready, when she had her life in order, when she had the safety and stability of her own home, then she would worry about passion. She used the edge of the sheet to blot the tears from her cheeks. She was a grown woman, not a teenager waiting to be swept away by passion; a smart woman who would never be swept away by love again if she had any say about it.

She had moved into the hills of northern Arizona precisely to get away from distractions, from other people's expectations, from the men—her brother, her father and her ex-husband—who had always overshadowed her life with their requirements, their plans. All in the name of love. She wasn't going to put aside her own needs to take care of someone else, to live someone else's life. And then watch them walk out the door. Never again.

"MOVE OVER, CARO." The whispered voice in Carolina's ear seemed familiar. A man's voice. Her body shifted on the bed in compliance even as her mind remained floating and puzzled, less than half awake. She sighed and relaxed against a solid, male torso as a warm hand slid leisurely along her stomach. Without any help from Carolina, her gown lifted and disappeared.

She was naked. And his hands were everywhere, touching, teasing, stroking her skin with fire. So slow and deliberate, it took her breath away. A murmur of words accompanied the movement, but she couldn't comprehend the meanings, couldn't grasp a thought. She arched her back and stretched as his fingers pushed between her thighs. So good . . . She wanted to move, to be still. She gasped a breath. She wanted . . .

His mouth, poised millimeters above her own, coaxed her further. "Open for me, Carolina. Let me—" Then he kissed her, sucking and tugging at her lips as she yielded.

He rolled over her then, settling his big body intimately upon her own. Carolina was beyond sadness and worry. Beyond sanity. She wanted this, all of it. And all of him. As he entered her with one emphatic thrust, Carolina's body rose naturally to meet his. To take, and to give. Her fingers dug into the taut muscles of his back to pull him downward.

"Will—"

A resounding crash reverberated through the cabin. Jolted out of her dazed pleasure, for a few terrifying seconds in the darkness Carolina didn't know where she was. Will. What was Will doing? A flash of pure fury cracked through her. She came fully awake, ready to fight. How dare he get into her bed!

But Will wasn't in her bed. A man his size would be difficult to overlook, even in the dark. Shoving her hair out of her eyes, Carolina had to admit to being alone, in her nightgown, as she had been when she'd gone to sleep. The digital clock on the night table read three-ten.

Another crash sounded at the front of the cabin, followed by the furious barking of a dog. With her heart

pumping in confusion and fear, Carolina stumbled out
of her room toward the noise.

A little more than halfway down the hall she ran
straight into a very large moving object. Will. Even
though she recognized him without the lights, the
shocking contact with his bare chest and the warm
musky smell of his skin accentuated her confusion. She
gasped and fell backward. His hands bracketed her
shoulders to steady her.

"What's going on?"

"I don't know," Carolina answered, breathless. The
so-real quality of her dream swept around her like a
scene from a half-forgotten movie. Being in Will's arms,
pulling him closer, wanting him . . . She couldn't think
of anything besides the need to get farther away.
Abruptly, she twisted out of his grasp and headed for
the stairs. "I'll turn on the front lights."

Will's fingers curled around her upper arm. "Wait.
I'll go."

Carolina wasn't arguing. She simply levered her arm
out of his restraining grip. "I'll turn on the lights, and
you can see what's happening."

The total darkness downstairs didn't slow her down.
Carolina knew the layout of the house. At the bottom
of the staircase she remembered to move right to avoid
the end table, her mind locked on getting to the front
door and the switch for the outside lights. The dog was
frantic, and there seemed to be a struggle taking place
on the front porch.

Carolina almost made it to the door. But her foot
caught and she slid, then stumbled, jamming her toes
against the solid weight of the couch.

"Ow! Ow, ow, ow, ow!" She grabbed her foot and
fell sideways. Tears flooded her eyes. "Ooowww."

"Carolina?" Will's concerned voice came from behind her, near the stairs. "Where are you?"

Carolina gulped back her pain and answered him. "On the couch."

"I can't see a damned thing." She heard something fall to the floor. "Where's the nearest light?"

"On the end table to your left."

In very short notice, the room was illuminated, and Will was bending over her. "Are you hurt?"

"Yes," she said, truthfully. She kept both her hands wound tightly around her toes. She was afraid to look. "I tripped and jammed my toes."

He dropped to one knee in front of her and reached for her foot. "Let me see."

Carolina's entire body blushed. Even the pain couldn't mitigate her embarrassment. Will was kneeling at her feet, half dressed—he had pulled on his jeans and zipped them, but the button was open—and she was in her thigh-length nightgown without a robe. The situation, combined with the dream she had so recently experienced made her want to cover her face and groan out loud.

A new round of barking broke out on the porch, giving Carolina the excuse she desperately needed. "See what's wrong with the dog," she said through clenched teeth. "A murderer could be trying to break into the house, and we'd be sitting here examining my toes."

Will didn't argue. He pushed to his feet and went to the front door. After switching on the outside lights, he yanked on the work boots he had left near the mat and turned the lock.

"Quiet down, Fang," he ordered.

As soon as Will stepped through the door and disappeared, Carolina began to worry. What if there really was someone out there? Will had no weapons. She struggled to stand, in case he might need help. Her toes hurt too much to step on her whole foot, so she limped across the room on her heel. It seemed to take a painful eternity to get to the front door.

The porch looked like a tornado had hit it. Two of her planters had been knocked over, and dirt was scattered everywhere. One of the chairs had been forced against the windows, the other rested on its side. Will was standing at the bottom of the stairs holding Fang's collar. Like the loser in a prizefight, Fang stood panting, his face all dirty. A bloody scratch marked one ear.

"It's a raccoon, I think," Will said, watching the animal scurry off into the trees.

Carolina wearily pushed the hair out of her eyes with a shaking hand. "A ringtail," she said. Her toes were throbbing like they would explode at any moment, her nerves were strung as tight as a violin string, and the very least of her worries, a ringtail, had been fended off.

"Great," she managed as tears came to her eyes again. She turned away from Will and limped into the living room.

She heard the scraping of chairs and the thump of wood being stacked. After a few minutes, Will entered the cabin. He switched off the outside light as he levered off his boots, then locked the front door and headed straight into the bathroom. He came out carrying a wet cloth in his hand. Carolina was curled up on the couch, gingerly testing her toes. She'd tried blowing on them, but that didn't seem to help. He kneeled in front of her once again.

"I'll clean up the rest of the mess in the morning." He offered a hand, palm up. "Let me see your toes." When she hesitated, he added, "I let you sear my scalp with alcohol. Come on, be good." He wiggled his fingers impatiently. "I'm an expert. Anyone who works with wood knows about smashed fingers and toes."

Carolina edged her gown down, then reluctantly extended her foot. When his fingers coiled around her instep, she flinched. "It really hurts, don't—"

He wrapped the cool cloth around her toes then squeezed with a steady pressure, almost enough to hurt but not quite. The throbbing pain began to subside.

"What did you fall over?" he asked, conversationally.

Carolina wanted to squirm, but now that the pain was easing, she decided to stay still. "Those damned boxes I moved out of your room," she confessed in disgust. She held up a hand to stop any comment. "I know. I've decided I've got too much stuff. I don't want the new house to be as crowded as this one."

A knowing curl of his lips made her heart turn over. He deftly removed the rag, refolded it and replaced the coolest part over her toes. "You'll have more room in the new house. I'll install a lot of cabinets and bookshelves so you can put most of this stuff away." The curl of his lips turned into a smile. His eyes drifted upward. "You look different with your hair loose."

Carolina watched him study her intently and waited for the punch line. But none came. Then realization struck like a bucket of cold water. Carolina winced and looked away. She must be a mess, with red eyes and straggling hair. She had to swallow and clear her throat before she could speak. "Will . . ." she began, unable to meet his eyes directly. She couldn't fight her reaction to his smile just then, not after the erotic dream of him in her arms in her bed. "I'm not so sure that this living together thing is going to work."

Will's smile disappeared, but his hands remained steady on her foot. "I'm sorry about Fang. I didn't think he could get into trouble so easily. I tied him to—"

"It's not just Fang." Carolina, trapped again by Will's questioning green eyes, searched for the words to explain it to him. How to say that she was attracted to him. No, extremely attracted to him. She couldn't—

She carefully pulled her foot out of his hands and forced a laugh. "I feel sort of . . . uncomfortable. Here we are, me in my nightgown and you—" Her gaze lowered to his bare chest, then skipped lower to the unfastened button on his jeans. Her explanation fizzled.

His features hardened into a frown. He crushed the wet cloth in one hand and got to his feet. "I'm not trying to come on to you, if that's what you're worried about."

Carolina stared at him, struggling with the sharp, unexpected pain reverberating deep inside her. Intellectually, she had known he wasn't interested in her as a woman. But to hear him say it hurt more than she'd foreseen. "I don't mean that," she said. *It's not you*, she wanted to say. It's me. She couldn't punish him for her own wayward emotions. "I don't feel that from you."

She bit her lip. He looked wounded and angry, as if she had slapped him. Why had she thought she could ever explain this?

"What did he do to you?"

Carolina blinked, wondering if she'd heard him correctly. "What did who—"

"Your ex-husband. What did he do to make you want to run away from everything, from everyone?"

"Will, he has nothing to do with—"

"You say you're not afraid of me, but you're afraid of something. Tell me I'm wrong." He propped one hand on his hip and waited.

Carolina stared at Will wondering how her personal fears and disappointments had become the topic of conversation. She wasn't about to discuss Paul with anyone, especially another man. Especially a younger man who would probably agree wholeheartedly with Paul's idea of the perfect woman—one who never changes. "We're all afraid of something," she said, sticking to generalities.

He stood frowning at her, a look of disappointment in his eyes. For a moment, locked with his gaze, Carolina weakened. The urge to get everything said rose inside her. She wanted to tell Will the truth about her confusion, about her surprise over her physical reaction to him. She wanted to laugh with him at the irony of her being attracted to a younger man after being dumped by her husband for a younger woman. Then the memory surfaced of the day she'd tried to explain the breakup of her marriage to her brother. Brad had gone crazy and punched a door, threatening to kill Paul. Very understanding and mature. And comforting.

"Never mind," she said finally, and gingerly stood up. It was her problem, not Will's. She would get through it on her own. When her balance faltered, he reached out, but hesitated before actually touching her. "I'm just tired. I'll get used to you and Fang," she promised.

To show him that she meant her words, she eased the weight on her foot by holding onto his upper arm and asked, "Would you help me up the stairs?" She knew she was going to cry again, and she wanted to be in her own room when it happened.

The stairway was too narrow for them to walk side by side. Looking more defiant than considerate, Will bent and slipped one arm around her back, the other under her thighs. Without a word, he lifted her, almost daring her to argue. They made it up without mishap. The level hallway posed no problem, but as they reached her bedroom door, Carolina felt Will hesitate again, as if he were treading on forbidden ground. He carefully lowered her feet to the floor, and she maneuvered forward on her own to switch on the lamp next to the bed. Her only thought was to lie down, pull the covers over her head and cry for the indignity of raging hormones and the dull throbbing of hurt toes. When she turned and sat on the edge of her mattress, she saw that Will was still standing in the doorway.

"Listen," he said, as he raked a hand through his hair. His lips tightened. "I'm sorry. For whatever you're mad about, I—"

"I'm not mad at you," Carolina confessed, and she was telling the truth. Everything would be so much simpler if she was mad at him. They could argue and get it over with. She could throw him out and tell her brother she'd tried. But she was angry with herself, not him or even his dog. Arguments careened through her thoughts like a carousel gone berserk, around and around, always ending in the same spot. She didn't want to throw him out. She needed her new house, and she needed Will to build it. But each moment they spent together seemed to test something inside her, and she was afraid she might fail the examination. If a perfect stranger could disrupt her peace of mind so drastically, she might find that all her well-chosen assumptions and

decisions about getting control of her life—or at least
finding some inner peace—were a joke.

Will braced an impatient hand on his hip. He looked
as though he wanted to argue, to force the truth out of
her. "Are you sure you're all right?"

"Yes," she answered automatically. Any other reply
would be an opening to discussion. She didn't want to
talk, or even watch him talk. "Good night," she said,
as sadness welled up inside her. She felt like such a fool.

He held her gaze for a brief moment, then turned to
leave.

"Will?"

He stopped.

"Would you close the door, please?" Carolina needed
more than half a hallway between them after her
dream. She needed time and space to restore her equilibrium.

Will looked angry again. "Sure," he said, and
reached for the doorknob. His eyes connected with hers
for a second, and she had the distinct impression that
he was going to ask if she wanted him to lock it, too.
But he didn't. "Good night," he added before soundly
shutting the door.

4

"I THINK I'm having a mid-life crisis," Carolina said into the phone.

Her friend Sue Ann had the audacity to laugh. "It's about time. You've been rational much too long to suit my peace of mind."

"I'm serious."

"I know, and that's what makes it funnier. So what is it? Are you behind schedule for the show?"

Carolina fiddled with a piece of gold wire she'd left on her workbench. She really should be working, if not with her jewelry, then at least on the drawer pulls for the new house. "No . . . Well, maybe a little, but work isn't the problem." She had to stop and choose her next words, too embarrassed to broadcast her overreaction to Will, even to Sue Ann. "Brad's friend is staying here, Will Case. The guy who's going to build the house."

"And . . . What?" Sue Ann prodded. "Is he weird or something?" Her voice took a more serious tone. "Are you worried about him?"

"N-no," Carolina stammered. "Not worried." She flinched at the lie. She was worried, but none of this was Will's fault. "He's fine," she added quickly. "I'm not used to having someone underfoot in the cabin. Especially a man." Especially a man who smiled like a wolf and didn't seem to own a T-shirt.

"You could get used to it. It's well past time for you to meet some new men. By the way, what does this Will guy look like?"

"Young." Carolina said the word as if it explained everything.

"And? Short, tall? Two eyes, one nose?"

"He's attractive," Carolina answered evasively. Deadly when he smiles, she revised silently.

"How young did you say he was?"

"I didn't, and don't start getting ideas. You have a husband you're crazy about, and I'm not going to follow in Paul's footsteps by chasing after younger men."

"I thought Paul liked younger women," Sue Ann teased.

"Very funny. You know what I mean."

Sue Ann laughed once more. "And, in case you haven't looked in the mirror lately, take my word for it, there aren't many men who would require a chase. Jimmy Kirkland would build a fence around all ten of your acres if you would just smile at him."

"I don't need a fence." And she didn't need Jimmy Kirkland. She was determined to put her love and energy into building her new home. She could trust a house to still be there in ten years.

"Well, maybe this Will guy is exactly what you do need. Someone to remind you that divorced doesn't mean dead."

Exactly what she needed? For a brief moment Carolina wondered if her friend had completely lost her mind, or if she'd been drinking. The last thing she needed was to take up with a younger man and have her nose rubbed in the fact that she was an older woman.

"When do I get to meet him?"

"You don't," she said, hoping to put Sue Ann off.

"Carolina!"

"All right, soon—" A knock sounded at her studio door. "Hang on a second." She stretched the phone cord to the door and opened it, causing the silver bell suspended from the frame to jingle. Will stood on the step. Carolina felt as though she'd swallowed her tongue. Had he been standing there long enough to hear her conversation? What had she said?

Seeing that Carolina was on the phone, Will raised a hand and mouthed, "I'll wait." But she waved him inside before turning her attention to her conversation.

As Will stepped through the doorway, his eyes automatically scanned the room. Carolina's studio was slightly less crowded than her house. He wondered at the difference between them. She surrounded herself, anchored herself, with things. Not symbols of money and success, just things she seemed to love and need, or things she used and wanted, or just things. He'd spent his life letting go of places and things... and people. As long as he had a new horizon, a new adventure and something to build—something that would last—he was happy.

Something like the Shinto temple. The goal that had been a shimmering mirage on the edge of his future for two years. Last summer, he'd been sure he'd be working in Japan by now. Instead he was in Arizona building a house for Carolina.

"Maybe next week when things have settled into a routine," Carolina said to the person on the other end of the line. Whatever she was promising, Will thought, she didn't sound too enthused. "I'll keep you posted," she added.

Will moved over to a frame leaning behind a stack of magazines. It held a photographic article on Carolina's work from a well-known art magazine. The slick, double-page spread showed several striking pieces of jewelry, labeled as original designs by Villada. Impressed, Will picked up the frame to get a closer look. Carolina was damned good. A curled piece of paper like the fortune out of a cookie protruded from the corner of the frame. He smoothed the paper and read, "No matter where you go, there you are."

"Did you need me for something?"

It took Will a moment to realize Carolina was speaking to him and that her phone conversation had ended. She breezed by him to hang up the receiver as if everything in the universe was sweetness and light. Like she wasn't limping slightly. Like his dog hadn't practically destroyed her front porch the night before. Like she had never looked at him apprehensively, as if he were trying to crawl between her thighs on the pretext of soothing her hurt foot.

He returned the frame in his hand to its leaning position. "The equipment to dig the foundation will be delivered this afternoon," he said. "I have to go into Prescott to meet the crew. Tomorrow morning, we start."

Carolina turned to face him. A real smile curved her mouth. "Great. Is there anything you need for me to do?"

Will had her complete interest now and had to remind himself that he should stick to business. The house. That's what she wanted from him. Nothing else. Not compliments, or conversation at dinner, or soothing hurt toes. Not discussing ex-husbands. He pushed his hands into the pockets of his jeans. "No," he answered. "We'll take it step-by-step and handle any problems as they come up. The crew I hired has a good rep. I just stopped to tell you I'm going into town in case you needed something."

He needed to get out of there. He was tired, and irritated that she always managed to make him feel like a ten-year-old facing the principal. No, he had to amend that. He hadn't felt like a ten-year-old the night before. After holding her in his arms, carrying her up the stairs to her bedroom, he'd suffered a savage attack of pure, old-fashioned, jaw-tightening, grown-up lust. The kind that made it difficult to sleep. The kind that made him want to forget the fact that she was Brad's sister—and too hung up on her ex-husband. The kind that goaded him to show her just how grown-up he was.

"Do you need directions?"

Will shook his head in silent disgust. He'd traveled and worked all over the world, and she was worried he'd get lost in Prescott, Arizona. "No. I can find it." He caught himself before adding a sarcastic, "Ma'am," and turned toward the door. *Stay out of her way and build the house, Will*, he chided himself. "See you later," he said aloud, then shut the door behind him like a good boy.

STANDING AT THE WORK site three days later, Carolina was amazed by the progress that had been made. The foundation was finished. The men on the crew were packing up equipment and loading it onto their trucks. Instead of an insubstantial dream, her house, her new beginning, stood in the first stages of becoming a reality, anchored in the ground by steel and concrete.

She spied Will talking to a man on the far side of an idling cement truck. He waved, and she moved in that direction.

The past three days, and nights, with Will in her house had been somewhat easier. He seemed determined to stay out of her way as much as possible, and she had welcomed the gesture. She'd made a set of rules concerning Will Case, and one of those rules was that she would only visit the house site once a day. That way she could get her own work done and keep the distance of an employer with an employee.

The self-imposed separation didn't help a lot. It only seemed to accentuate her reaction when she did see him. But she had to do something. She'd caught herself thinking about him more times than she would ever admit. Will was leaning against the back of his truck, laughing at something the man he was talking to had said. With each step toward him, Carolina's pulse took a leap in rhythm. The feeling was wonderful and scary, and each time she experienced it, she wondered just how long hormonal responses were supposed to last.

"Hey, boss lady," Will said and smiled.

"Hi," she managed.

"This is an old timber-framing friend of mine—" he indicated the man standing with him "—Michael Graham. Mike, this is the boss around here, Carolina Villada."

As Carolina shook hands with Mike, Will continued, "Mike is going to help me do the actual shaping and framing. I called the shipper, and the timbers should be delivered on Monday."

"Do you live around Prescott?" Carolina asked.

"No," Mike answered. "I'm from Pennsylvania."

"Long way from home."

"Well, I'm used to being on the road. Timber framers are sort of like gypsies, married to the world and to the next job."

"Don't tell that to his wife," Will injected. "How many kids do you have now?"

Mike looked a little sheepish. "Two," he answered.

Will shook his head in mock disgust. "Let's see, the last convention I went to was in Vermont. What was that? About three years ago? I remember you saying you would never do the 'one-woman thing' even though Laura was on your case. Now you're an old married man with a family. You probably can't even play a decent game of volleyball anymore." Will crossed his arms and sighed.

Carolina inwardly flinched at the word *old*. Mike Graham couldn't be more than a few years older than Will, and certainly not her age. She smiled at Mike to conceal her reaction.

Mike laughed and retorted, "You set up a net and we'll see. We have a national convention for our heavy timber guild once a year," he explained to Carolina. "This guy—" he tilted his head toward Will "—has only managed to be there twice. Both times he ended up on the winning volleyball team. But I know how to beat him." He nodded sagely.

"How's that?" Will challenged with a disbelieving smirk.

Mike winked at Carolina before taunting Will with his answer. "Beer."

Carolina laughed and looked at Will. Big mistake. He was smiling, and when their eyes met, the whole scene drifted into slow motion for Carolina. She had no idea what was happening, but as she watched, Will's good-natured grin seemed to falter slightly, the mischievous glint in his eyes turning serious in the next heartbeat. Carolina was caught, completely, and she had no idea how to extract herself. After what seemed like five minutes of unidentified flying communication between them, Will shifted his attention to his friend.

"You can't afford that much beer," he quipped. To Carolina, his voice sounded different. Or was it just the buzzing in her ears? Mike didn't seem to notice. Carolina decided her imagination had gone berserk along with her hormones.

"You drag your sorry butt to the next one in San Antonio and we'll see. I can take up a collection for the beer."

Men were starting cars and trucks and leaving the area. One of the workers yelled, "See ya!" Will waved in response.

Mike glanced at his watch. "I guess I better get on the road, too," he said.

Carolina's senses were beginning to return to normal. "Where are you staying?" she asked.

"My wife has a cousin who lives about thirty miles from civilization on the other side of Prescott. I'm staying with his family." He turned to Will. "If you need help prepping I could come out tomorrow, then we'll be all set when the sticks get here."

"Don't you want to spend some time visiting your cousin?" Will prodded devilishly.

Mike didn't blink an eye. "Not if I can avoid it."

The two men laughed again and Will said, "Sure, come on out. I can use any help I can get."

"Nice to meet you," Mike said to Carolina. "And thanks for the job. Will and I have worked together before. We'll build you one heck of a frame. See you tomorrow."

After Mike's car rumbled away, quiet descended on the deserted work site. Will had done a full, hard day's work, and he felt more like himself. And it was good to see Mike again. But, he thought, disgruntled, he still hadn't acquired the skill of keeping his thoughts off Carolina. Alone with her once again, Will stretched, then straightened from his leaning stance and took her arm. "Come on," he said and led her toward the new foundation. After helping her step over the fresh concrete, he released her. "You are now standing in your new living room. What do you think?"

Carolina studied the broken ground littered with pieces of two-by-fours and wayward globs of concrete. "Looks great," she answered. "I think."

Will took a deep breath and rested his hands on his hips. "It will be. This is just the beginning. I love this design. The way it goes together. Wait till you see it with the frame up." He didn't bother hiding his enthusiasm about the house. It was one area he knew interested Carolina, and he was telling the truth. He intended to build this exact house for himself someday. It pleased him that she had fallen in love with the plan, too.

He turned her and aimed her toward another section of the foundation, which had pipes sticking up in several places. "Your new kitchen," he informed her. "It makes the one you have now look like a closet."

"At least the one I have now has walls," Carolina countered, but she was smiling again. He liked that. When she had looked at him earlier, laughing, he'd felt like when he was a kid and he'd touched the refrigerator while standing on a wet part of the floor. Electrified. In that one crazy millisecond, when she'd gazed at him, he'd nearly pulled her into his arms, in front of Mike and in spite of her lack of interest. He knew how to generate interest. . . .

"Where's the bathroom? Here?" She asked, as she stepped toward another group of pipes.

"Right," he answered. "You know, you could have plumbing put in for a hot tub on the deck if you want."

"Hot tub?" Carolina frowned. "That's so California..."

"It brings some interesting possibilities to mind," Will added before he could stop himself. "Watching the sunset with a friend..."

Carolina turned to face him with a perfectly blank look, but he could see the color rising in her cheeks. He shrugged and laughed. "Sorry, I couldn't resist. Seriously, it wouldn't be difficult to do at this stage. Maybe you could barter for it."

Carolina pivoted and walked a few more feet away from him. "I'll think about it," she said as she closely studied another section of the foundation.

I'll think about it too, Will mused disconsolately. He'd already been thinking about it, more than he should have, and the friend he'd envisioned her watching the first sunset with was standing in his boots. He would enjoy showing her some of the strategic gravity advantages enjoyed by two bodies submersed in water.

In the next moment, Will purposely clamped down on that scenario. Brad would go ballistic if he knew what Will had been contemplating about Carolina. And she would probably make him sleep in his truck. Will rubbed a hand along the back of his neck. It was just as well that she wasn't open to any of his suggestions. He didn't want to antagonize the whole family. It didn't hurt to imagine, though... except sometimes in the middle of the night. Then, it hurt like hell.

Carolina nudged a loose piece of wood with her toe. "So, do you feel like they did a good job?"

Will had to force his mind to the subject at hand—the house. "Yeah," he answered. "I know it looks a little messy, but they did it right." He dragged a red handkerchief from his back pocket and wiped his dusty face. "Well, I guess I'll go untie Fang, then get cleaned up." He shoved the bandanna into his pocket. He'd felt guilty about tying the dog up with these great woods to run around in. But, if he hadn't kept Fang out of the way, the dumb dog would probably be covered with wet concrete.

Carolina fell into step next to him on the trail to the cabin. "He's been depressed all day. I gave him one of those giant dog biscuits you bought," she confessed. "I hope you don't mind."

"I don't mind," he said, making an effort to hide his grin. "Food always cheers me up. It probably works that way for him, too."

Later, after dinner, Carolina made herself a cup of tea and took it out on the porch. The air had a spring coolness to it even though they were headed into summer. The sun had fallen behind the hump of the mountains, but its apricot-tinged light still colored the sky. Fang trotted over to give her a greeting as she sat down on the top stair. She drew in a deep breath and absently patted the dog's head. Even though it seemed like her daily routines had changed drastically in the past week, Carolina realized she felt good about it. She'd managed to complete several new pieces of jewelry for the first show, her house was under way, and she was even getting used to Fang. She heard the door behind her open, then close as Will followed her out.

"This is the perfect time of day," he said. He pulled one of the oversize wooden chairs on the porch a little closer to Carolina and sat down.

Fang gave Carolina's hand one farewell swipe with his tongue then hiked himself up the steps to flop down next to Will. "I think so, too," she said as she propped her back against the post and turned toward him. Will's hair was still slightly damp from the shower he'd taken before dinner. His shirt was buttoned but not tucked into his jeans. With his long legs stretched out in front of him, crossed at the ankles, he was the perfect picture of a domesticated male.

But Carolina knew he wasn't tame. Domestication implied being settled in one place, and Will was a traveler. Her mind touched on a long-forgotten dream of starting out in life, of building a house and a future side by side with a man. A dream she'd outgrown when Paul left.

"It's so quiet here," Will said, then looked at her. "Aren't you ever afraid, living alone so far away from your neighbors?"

Carolina set down her teacup, drew one knee up and wrapped her arms around it. She scanned the surrounding trees as if seeing them for the first time. "No," she said after a moment. She couldn't stop a smile. "This place has always been my refuge. Like some of the new agers over in Sedona say, this is my power place." Her smile faded. "Seriously, I feel good here. Strong. Not afraid." Not until you showed up, she added silently. Somehow Will had set the whole view of her organized life on end. Just when she'd decided that she could do without a man, Will had walked through the door and made her knees weak with merely a smile. Just when she thought she'd come to terms with not being twenty something anymore, Will had made her wish she could turn back the clock. And that terrified her.

Carolina was determined not to cry over the past or waste the rest of her life wishing she was younger.

"Don't you get lonely?" At the sound of Will's voice, Fang stirred, sat up and flopped his chin on Will's thigh. Carolina watched Will's large hand run over the top of the dog's head.

"I have friends," she answered evasively. She picked up her cup and took a sip of tea to ease the tightening of her throat. She didn't want to talk about loneliness, or the past, or second chances. What good would it do?

"I mean men friends. Isn't there anyone who's a little nervous about me staying here?"

"Just me," Carolina said without thinking, then immediately wanted to bite her tongue. Why had she said that? Her eyes slanted anxiously toward Will. His hand had stopped moving suddenly. He was staring at her in an alert, speculative way. She needed damage control. "I, uh—"

The ringing of the telephone rescued her. "I'll get it," she said unnecessarily and pushed up from her seat on the stairs to go inside. She felt as though she'd been saved by the bell. If she'd had to explain her remark to Will, God knows what she might have confessed.

"Hi, Sis. How's it going?"

"Fine," Carolina answered as she coped with the erratic pounding of her heart. *Even though I'm losing my mind,* she thought.

"Fine? That's it?" Brad sounded worried. "How is the house coming along? Is Will there?"

"Yes." She turned toward the door as Will came through it. "He's here. It's Brad," she said, then handed the phone to Will and headed for the kitchen.

Will watched Carolina walk away, and for the first time the thought that she was running from him surfaced. What the hell did that mean? "Hey, buddy," he said into the phone, "what's up?"

"Nothing much here. What's happening out there? Has my sister been bustin' your chops?"

"No, she's fine." Now there was an understatement if he'd ever made one.

Carolina remained suspiciously scarce during the rest of the conversation. Will filled Brad in on the new foundation they'd put in for the house and talked about the framing.

"It's hard to believe my sister's not giving you a hard time. But, then again, she admires good work and I know you build a hell of a house."

"Thanks, man," Will replied.

"Run across any interesting women yet?"

Carolina chose that moment to return from the kitchen. Will had to stifle the true comment he'd like to make—that he was looking at one. "No, haven't had time."

"I'm sure you'll get around to it." Brad laughed.

Will watched Carolina walk across the room and curl up on the couch. "I'm sure I will," he said. The sooner the better for everyone concerned, he decided. Just hearing Brad's voice put a damper on his lecherous thoughts concerning his best buddy's sister. For a moment, when they were sitting on the porch, she'd looked fragile again. He wasn't going to screw around with her, or her life.

"I'm going to try to make it out there before the house is finished. Maybe we can check out the females together. I'm training a new manager so I can take some time off."

"That'll be great. I might even put you to work. Real work, not pushing a bar towel or counting liquor bottles." Will's gaze remained on Carolina. He wished for the hundredth time that she wasn't Brad's sister. That he didn't know how badly she'd been hurt.

"Well, don't tell Caro this, but owning a sports bar is a lot more work than I thought it would be. Even if I do get to watch all the games on a big-screen TV."

"Tough life," Will teased. "You want to speak to Brad again?" he asked Carolina.

"Sure." She held her hand out for the phone.

"Take it easy, man," he said to Brad and surrendered the receiver to her.

Will listened as they talked about family things—parents and past history. Then he felt Carolina's attention shift to him.

"He's okay," she said, sounding wary. "No—" her gaze fell away from his "—no problems." She smiled halfheartedly. "He's a lot neater than you are." Her smile brightened a bit. "I know, you had a difficult childhood, living with a sister like me. But I don't think you can use that excuse for too many more years." She laughed. "Yeah, right. You do the same. Bye."

Will moved around a chair to take the receiver from her and hang up the phone. As he returned to sit across from her, he noticed some of the boxes she had fallen over a few nights before had been moved and opened.

Carolina lifted her foot in the direction of the closest one. "You want to hear something funny?"

Will leaned back and waited.

"I finally opened those boxes to see if I could throw out some things and I found that two of them are full of my ex-husband's books."

The muscles in Will's shoulders tensed. He had never heard anything funny when an ex-husband was connected to it. "And?" he managed, determined to sound interested.

She shrugged. "I don't know. I thought it was funny. It's sort of like one of those cosmic kicks in the pants that remind you to clear up your old business. The best thing about tripping over those boxes is that now I can tape them up and ship them out to L.A. I don't have to look for a place to store them. And I won't ever trip over them again." She raised her foot and wiggled it.

"Do you hear from him much?"

"Who? Paul?"

Will didn't really want to know his name. Better to think of him as a nameless, faceless, asshole. "Yeah," he managed, working for an innocent, inquiring look. "Paul—your ex."

"No, not often."

Brad's words echoed, "The guy bailed out on her and she still loves him!" Will watched Carolina's expression shift from smiling to wary but he couldn't stop the words. "The best way to get over someone is to find someone else." He softened the advice with a glimpse of his own battle. "Believe me, I've been there."

Her chin lifted. She stared at him for a long moment but she didn't look receptive or convinced. "There's nothing to get over," she said, and crossed her arms over her chest. The lie was so obvious he couldn't help calling her on it.

"Nothing, huh? Brad said—"

"Brad!" She laughed, but with more nervousness than humor. "Brad doesn't know anything about—"

The phone rang.

"I haven't had this many calls since I moved here," she complained as she got up to answer it, but she looked relieved. "Hello. Oh, hi, Mike. Yes, he's here."

She offered the receiver to Will. "Sounds like he's at a party."

Carolina listened as Will made plans to meet Mike. Saved by the phone again. She said a silent thank you to Alexander Graham Bell and to Mike. The personal nature of her conversation with Will made her nervous. Why was he so interested in Paul? Was he trying to play big brother? Or amateur psychologist? A wave of embarrassment ran through her. What had Brad told him? That she'd been dumped by her husband for a younger model and he felt sorry for her?

"Do you know where the Square Peg Tavern is?" Will asked her.

Carolina could hardly look at Will. The image of Brad telling him some melodramatic tale of her marriage and divorce was too mortifying. She didn't need anyone's pity, especially Will's. "It's downtown. The old Whisky Row section on the square."

"Yeah. Okay. We know where it is," he said into the phone. "All right, see you in a bit." Will hung up and began to tuck his shirt into his jeans. He smiled one of his killer smiles. "Grab your shoes, boss lady. I'm going to buy you a beer."

Carolina's heart took several heavy beats. "You don't need me to show you where the bar is, I can tell you how to get there." Her voice came out careful, cool. Nothing like the singing chaos running around inside her chest. How did he do it? she wondered. How could he make her feel this way with merely a smile?

Will stopped arranging his shirt and rested his hands on his hips. He didn't look like someone who would take no for an answer. "You need to get out of this cabin." He nudged one of her shoes toward her with his foot. "Besides, a couple of beers or maybe a shot of tequila will make you sleep better."

Carolina's pounding heart paused midbeat. "How do you know I don't sleep well?" She asked, shocked by his perception.

He frowned, then walked over to the door to pick up his boots. "Because I can hear you moving around at night."

Carolina pulled on her shoes because she didn't know what else to do with her hands. And she didn't know what to say. The thought of him lying awake, listening to her toss and turn, made her feel even more vulnerable, exposed. As she stood to face him, she realized how dangerous this was. She didn't want to get to know him better, to get relaxed and friendly, to tell him about Paul. She didn't want to know that if she was wide awake at two-thirty in the morning, all she had to do was say his name and he would answer.

She groped for an excuse to leave for a moment, to think. "Let me rebraid my hair." Her words were low and hesitant. Emotional. She turned away from his steady gaze and walked into the bathroom.

THE BAR WAS SMOKY, the jukebox was loud and the stools were already half-full when they arrived. Several men in cowboy hats, along with a few women, were gathered around the two pool tables in the front. One couple was dancing on the scuffed, wooden dance floor in front of a small stage.

"The band starts playing in about thirty minutes," Mike said as he guided them over to a place he had staked out at the bar. "They're supposed to be pretty good."

Will nodded then turned to Carolina. He pulled a stool out for her to sit down. "What are you drinking?"

He had leaned close to her so that she could hear him over the music. The clean smell of his skin drifted to her. It seemed so natural to bend toward him. "Beer, I guess."

He straightened and caught the bartender's attention. Carolina gazed around the room. People, like the ones here kicking back after a long day's work, were one of the things she loved about this part of Arizona. No hundred-dollar neckties or fifteen-hundred-dollar ostrich-skin boots in this bar. Many of the folks who lived in Prescott still worked on ranches, ran cattle and trained horses. Her eyes shifted to Will. He fit right in, even though he wasn't wearing a cowboy hat. His jeans were faded and well worn, and his hands had calluses and skinned knuckles instead of manicured nails.

Carolina curled her own fingers inward. Paul had always encouraged her to have manicures to keep her hands nice. Hammering metals and working with chemicals and polishing wheels was not exactly dainty work. Like most of the people in the bar, her hands were strong but not model-pretty.

One of Will's long-fingered hands presented her with a frosty glass of beer. He clinked his glass to hers. "To your house." He included Mike in the toast.

Carolina took a sip of beer and smiled. "It's a little early to celebrate."

"Nah." Mike laughed. "We celebrate getting through each day. Timber framers have to stay in the right *frame* of mind."

Carolina rolled her eyes.

Will shook his head sorrowfully, but he was smiling. "Man, that was bad. Really bad."

"I almost forgot," Mike said, slapping a palm to his forehead as if to change channels. "I meant to ask you about this earlier today. I ran into an old buddy of yours in Massachusetts about a year ago. Tom Shelby. He said you were finally putting together a proposal for a project in Japan. What happened with it?"

Sitting on a bar stool sandwiched between them, Carolina felt like an eavesdropper—not required to participate. She watched Will take a long pull from his beer and frown before answering. A moment before, he'd been laughing.

"We sent letters of recommendation and photos of the work we'd done. We got a polite 'received your materials' kind of response. Then, nothing."

Mike leaned toward Carolina. "I can't imagine this guy—" he jerked a thumb in Will's direction "—volunteering to shave wood for six months. The Japanese are masters of joinery, but a normal apprenticeship lasts for years. They make the apprentice practice each phase over and over again before they let him actually build something." Mike shook his head. "They couldn't pay me enough."

Will set his beer on the bar with a thud. In a tone that sounded too serious for the occasion, he said, "I would've done it for nothing." He met Carolina's eyes for a brief moment. "I built a boat with an old-timer from Japan, and in the time I spent working with Naguro in California I learned more about wood than if I'd built twenty houses. Not the engineering of sixty-foot spans, or the physics of the bending moment, but the spirit and movement in the wood itself. The personality or workability of each tree, from the heart out."

Mike merely shrugged. Carolina was stunned. Listening to Will talk about his work in terms she might have used for her art made her realize she'd underestimated him. She'd judged him unfairly, thinking him like her brother. Brad's concept of the spiritual revolved around what kind of beer to order during happy hour.

"Besides, it wouldn't have been an apprenticeship. I was offering a partnership. I wanted to be a part of building a temple, something from my hands that would inspire and be revered long after I'm in the ground."

"Well, I can't afford to devote months of my life to the study of wood, or a contribution to posterity." Mike said. "I've got to work on jobs that pay the bills. Like this one," he added with a smile in Carolina's direction. Her eyes were on Will.

He shifted out of his serious demeanor, as if he'd said more than he'd intended. "I need to call Tom. What were you and he building in Massachusetts?" he asked.

Will and Mike spent several minutes catching up on news about several mutual friends and their latest projects. Someone turned off the jukebox and the band began tuning up, preparing for their first set. Several more people had drifted in through the front door, and many of the tables were filled.

Carolina had finished one beer and Will had ordered her another when she decided she needed to visit the ladies' room. She slid off the stool and spoke to Will. "I'll be back."

Will watched Carolina walk away. He couldn't help but admire her backside. The jeans she wore weren't too tight, they were just snug enough in the right places. He noticed that a few other men turned to watch her walk by, and an unfamiliar pang of ownership raced through

him. It startled him. He chalked it up to protective-
ness. Natural enough. She was Brad's sister, after all.

He returned to his conversation with Mike, although he made sure they didn't discuss Japan. He
didn't want to ruin his mood altogether. It had been
months since he'd finally faced the fact that he wasn't
going to hear good news from the Tashimo proposal.
Hell, he hadn't heard any news. Right now, he had
Carolina's house to build and that would keep him
busy. He'd find another way to work in Japan.

As he sipped his beer, he glanced occasionally in the
direction Carolina had disappeared. There were a few
other attractive women in the place, but most of them
had big hair and too much makeup. Will decided he'd
rather look at Carolina.

The band turned up the level of sound as they played
what was obviously a favorite two-step tune. Couples
were filling and circling the dance floor. Will saw Carolina emerge from the darkened hallway at the back of
the room. He saw her eyes search for him at the bar. Just
as their gaze connected, a man stepped in front of her
and touched her arm.

Of all the people in Prescott to run into, Carolina
thought as she stared at the man in front of her. For
months Jimmy Kirkland had hinted at, and joked
about, and then finally asked her out. And she'd declined.

There was nothing really wrong with him. Slightly
taller than she, he had a stocky build and craggy features. He looked like he'd worked hard most of his life,
and the peppering of silver in his dark hair alluded to
the fact that he was a few years older than she.

Sue Ann had proclaimed him the perfect start for
Carolina. But Carolina had a decided lack of enthusi-

asm for starting anything and had put him off. Too close to her divorce, too much work to do. Now, here she was—out. Without any of her excuses.

"I'm surprised to see you here. I thought you were too busy to party."

"Well, I . . ." Carolina casually moved away from his hand on her arm. "I . . ." She blinked and Will was standing on the other side of her.

His hand circled her wrist and tugged as if Jimmy Kirkland was an invisible man. "Come on, boss lady. You promised to show me how to do this dance." For a split second she almost planted her feet. But she couldn't tell if Will was being overbearing or playful. And she didn't mind being saved from making more lame excuses to Jimmy. After a helpless shrug and a smile in Jimmy's direction, she allowed Will to pull her toward the crowded dance floor.

"What was that about?" she asked as he took her other hand and shifted her into the sliding steps in time with the music. "And when did I promise to teach you to dance?" It was a moot question, since they were already moving with the other dancers. He obviously knew the two-step.

He leaned back to look into her eyes. He didn't appear playful. "Was that guy bothering you?"

"Bothering me?" He sounded like her father or her brother—typical, domineering male. Her gratitude at being saved chilled. "I'm a grown woman. I can *probably*— " great emphasis on probably "—take care of myself."

His frown remained. "I brought you here. I'm not going to let anyone hit on you, unless . . ." His expression changed slightly. "Did you want to talk to him?"

Carolina stared at him for a long moment, trying to sift through the currents of their conversation. She appreciated his concern, but she refused to allow him to take over her life. She picked up the thread of their earlier, too-personal conversation and used it against him.

"You told me I needed to get out of the house. That I needed to meet some men."

Will stopped dancing. Couples detoured around them as he held her stationary. "Do you want to go talk to him?" He loosened his grip on her but didn't pull away.

Embarrassed, Carolina pushed to get him started dancing again. "No, I don't." He moved into the circling dancers. "But it isn't up to you who I talk to or what I decide to do."

He didn't speak for one full revolution on the dance floor. "Fair enough," he said finally as the song ended. His hands released hers, and he waited for her to precede him to the bar.

"I ordered you a tequila shooter," Mike said to Will as Carolina regained her position on the bar stool. Will decided that his friend should become a fortune-teller. At that moment he needed a stiff kick. What was wrong with him? It was none of his business who Carolina talked to.

And he'd even suggested that she needed to meet another man. Yet when he'd seen a man touch her, he'd simply reacted. He glanced sideways at her. She'd told him to mind his own business. Why did that piss him off?

He pointed to the shot glass of tequila. "You want to try one of these?"

She wrinkled her nose. "I don't think so."

He casually raised his hand and ran his tongue across the back of it before sprinkling some salt on the spot. In one smooth action he licked the salt from his skin, downed the tequila then sucked on the piece of lime served with it.

The music was so loud he had to lean over close to her ear to make sure she heard him. "Chicken," he challenged. "How long has it been since you let go of that control a little?"

The look on her face was priceless. First surprise, then anger, then determination. He knew he shouldn't push her, but something seemed to be pushing him. He wanted to see her loose and feminine and smiling. In his direction.

Her back straightened. "One of us has to drive, you know." She sounded like a schoolteacher.

He leaned close again. He liked the way she smelled. "I tell you what. If you want to try a shooter or two...or three, I'll switch to ginger ale." He pulled back to look into her eyes. He wished she would laugh and lean into him. He wished she trusted him enough to relax. "I got you here, I'll get you home."

Carolina stared at Will as the song ended. She didn't mind being teased, but she didn't like being tested. She turned to catch the bartender's attention, ordered a tequila shooter and paid for it with the twenty-dollar bill she had stuck in her back pocket. Will nudged Mike's arm to get his attention but never took his amused gaze from her.

Caught somewhere between defiance and playfulness, Carolina kept her movements deliberate and slow. As she licked the back of her hand before applying the salt, she watched the amusement disappear from Will's green eyes. She held up the glass in a toasting gesture, smiled and downed the contents. The lime took the sting out of the liquor burning its way down her throat. Her chest felt like she had swallowed a glowing coal. The pain was worth it, however, because Will actually looked surprised.

Then he smiled. "One more for the lady," he told the bartender. "And I'll have ginger ale."

Mike laughed and clapped Carolina on the shoulder. She knew her face was red, a combination of newly born bravado and the silliness of taking a dare like a teenager. But she laughed. It felt good—the music, the dancing, sparring with Will. Even Jimmy Kirkland's attention was one step better than sitting at home. Why didn't she go out more? she wondered. This was fun.

When the bartender set the next shot of tequila in front of her, along with the requisite wedge of lime, common sense kicked in. The warmth in her chest had migrated downward and outward, relaxing and numbing as it went. If she drank another straight shot, she might not be able to stand. In answer to Will's questioning look, she shrugged and said, "I think I'll wait awhile. I want to make sure I can walk out of here."

He nodded, unconcerned, then turned to watch the dancers. Carolina followed his gaze. About twenty people were doing a line dance, stepping and swaying and kicking. Most of the dancers were women, young women, and every man in the room seemed to be entranced by the display. The dancers ranged from innocent fun-seekers to provocative show-offs, wearing tight jeans or short shorts, cowboy-style shirts or midriff-hugging crop tops. There was something for every female connoisseur in the room. Carolina wondered which woman Will preferred. The blonde in the red jeans or the brunette in the fringed skirt? She wanted to watch but she also wanted to be invisible. If learning a provocative dance routine to do for your man was the new trend in dating, she might as well stay home. She didn't own a pair of jeans tight enough.

At closer range, the bar was crowded with men and a few couples. Out of the corner of her eye, Carolina watched a woman wearing cutoff jeans and red cowboy boots make her way along the aisle near the bar. After patting one man she was clearly acquainted with on the shoulder, she moved closer. She had a ten-dollar bill in her hand, and her eyes were on Will.

"Excuse me," the woman said as she nudged Will's arm. Carolina watched him turn to her, watched the woman moisten her lips before she smiled at him with an invitation as ancient as Eve. "Can I squeeze in here and get a beer please?" Carolina looked away and didn't hear Will's reply. Her attention was glued to the dancers. She felt him shift so that the woman could get to the bar and wished she'd stayed home where she belonged.

The song ended on a loud jarring note, and Carolina decided not to think about whatever she had missed by spending the past ten years living her life for Paul. She didn't want to start over again, to try to act like she was twenty. She wanted safety—no more painful surprises.

Carolina felt a hand touch her arm. The band had begun a slow song. Will spoke close to her ear. "Dance with me."

The warmth from the tequila blossomed anew, and for a moment her pride pleaded that she say no. *Keep your distance and he can't hurt you.* But she wanted to dance, to feel his arms around her just once. Will gently but determinedly pulled her from the stool. Not demanding . . . enticing. Before she could look at him or force an answer through her lips, she was stepping onto the dance floor and moving into his arms.

Unlike during the two-step, there was no respectable distance between them. Will placed his hand over hers and rested it on his chest as he pulled her body against his. He was so warm. Carolina's other hand automatically looped over his shoulder at the base of his neck. Instead of pressing her face into his shirt, she angled it upward to rest her temple against his jaw. He began to move with the music, and Carolina's limbs followed his as if her brain had switched to autopilot. His other hand, at the small of her back, guided her movement, urging her one way, then another.

Carolina could hardly breathe. Every one of her senses seemed to be working overtime. Yet, she couldn't have testified as to what the singer was singing if her life depended on it. Her body was alive and warm everywhere their bodies touched. She wanted to melt against his chest and be surrounded by his arms. She wanted to breathe in the scent of soap on his skin. She wanted him to touch her in any way that would bring her closer. When the pad of his thumb drifted over the back of her hand exactly where she had licked the salt from her skin, the vision of his mouth, his tongue tasting the same spot sent a feathery chill along the fine hairs at the back of her neck. As if he had touched her there.

She missed a step. Will held her steady and with a low laugh said, "You either need another shot of tequila, or you need to be taken home and put to bed."

Words bloomed into fantasies—Will putting her to bed. That woke her up. What in the world was she doing? She gingerly pushed out of such close quarters and looked him in the eye. "I think I should go home."

He looked surprised. "Hey, I was just kidding." He smiled and reached to draw her back.

"No, really." She raised a hand toward the crowded dance floor. "There are plenty of other women to dance with here." And one at the bar interested in more than dancing, her mind taunted. "If you'll give me a ride home, you can come back."

One large hand slipped around her upper arm as she started to turn away. "Carolina? What's wrong?"

What's wrong? she wanted to shout. *You're too young, you're too sexy, you're too important to my house right now. I don't want to want you!*

But she did want him. The truth of it was staring her in the face, breathing down her neck. She couldn't believe he was seriously trying to seduce her. Not with all these other available women around. But whether he was or he wasn't, her pride couldn't let him see how foolishly easy it would be. How could she ever hold the interest of a man like Will? And how could she stand to watch another man leave her?

She angled out of his grip and conjured up a smile. "It's okay. I'm not used to this, remember?" In her haste to get away, she backed into another couple lost in the music. The young man stumbled against her, turned, nodded politely and said, "Excuse me, ma'am." Carolina stared at him, feeling frozen inside. *Ma'am.* Ma'am was something you said to your mother or your high school teacher. God. She had to get out of there. Will was frowning as she latched on to his arm and hauled him from the dance floor.

They said goodbye to Mike and they were almost to the door when Jimmy Kirkland appeared in front of

Carolina again. He nodded good-night and, as she walked by, said, "I'll call you."

Carolina nodded back, which seemed the only brief thing to do, then she stepped out into the night.

5

THEY DROVE for several miles without conversation. Will kept his attention on the road, and Carolina looked out the side window of his truck. Unspoken questions crackled like radio static in the air between them. Carolina fought the confusion and sadness running around inside her, unleashed by a few drinks and a few dances with an attractive young man. Confusion over how to diffuse the emotions Will set in motion by his mere presence, and sadness because the divorce had shattered her illusions. She'd suddenly had to grow up and face reality. Thanks to Paul. And now she couldn't even pretend to believe in vows or second chances.

She also fought the frustration. Her body was so alive that each place her clothes touched her skin seemed like torture. She wanted Will. She wished she could be young and beautiful—the perfect woman—for him. For one night.

"I'm not letting you out of this truck until you tell me what's wrong." Will's voice held no amusement.

Carolina's body tensed even more. "What do you mean?"

He glanced at her. "I mean, I've got a full tank of gas. I can drive around all night." He paused for several seconds. "I want to know why one moment you're laughing and dancing, and the next moment you want to go home."

Their progress was stopped by a red light at a cross-roads that seemed to be in the middle of nowhere. Carolina could feel Will's gaze on her, but she couldn't face him. She stared at the dashboard, at her hands—anywhere.

"Look at me . . . please." The command became an entreaty.

Carolina met his eyes and saw concern, not anger. She let out the breath she'd been holding. "You must think I'm crazy or something," she managed.

The light turned green and Will started the truck forward again.

"You tell me what to think."

Get it over with. Tell him. Tell him what? The embarrassing truth? That she was human and female and whether or not she was older, she wanted him just like several other women in the bar tonight had wanted him. But she couldn't afford to put her newfound peace on the firing line for one night of fantasy. For one attractive young man's attention. The very thought made her stomach skitter uneasily. It had nearly killed her to come to grips with the idea of Paul with his new, young woman, sharing all the intimacies and plans of a couple while she had to put her life back together alone. She'd had enough rejection to last a lifetime.

"I, uh. . . It's been awhile since I've been. . ." She could feel his gaze again and sighed. Even the truth was too humiliating. "I don't want to give you the wrong signals."

"Signals?"

"The wrong idea of what I want from you." She grasped her older-sister persona and turned toward him. "We can be friends but tonight, the dancing . . ." She swallowed as she thought of his arms around her, his chest— "I know you think I'm lonely but...I'm fine. You don't have to worry about me. Or try to entertain me."

Will went silent again, and his features settled into a frown. His eyes slanted to hers. "What's wrong with having a good time?" he asked, finally. "Weren't you having a good time?"

Carolina looked out the side window once more. They were turning onto the road to the cabin. A good time. If Will was a stranger and not her brother's best friend, not the man building her house, maybe she could find the nerve to have a good time. But he wasn't and she couldn't. "It was...different," she said, gathering her acting talents. "It's been years since I've spent any time hanging out in bars." Was that condescending enough? she wondered. Take the hint, Will, and leave it alone.

He pulled the truck up in front of the cabin and switched off the engine.

Carolina's hand itched to open the door, to escape whatever was coming. Sitting in a car, in the dark, in the woods. The thought of him simply reaching out and touching her made her pulse drum in her ears.

"You don't like bars?" His voice was calm, detached.

Shrugging nonchalantly, Carolina answered, "They're fine...for young people who are..."

He shifted on the seat to face her and leaned his shoulder against the door. His face, half in shadow, half in light from the cabin, looked perfectly calm and absolutely dangerous at the same time. She couldn't see the unusual green of his eyes, but she could feel his intense gaze zeroing in on her. "Young people who are what?"

"Who are dating," she answered in exasperation.
"Who are looking for—" A lover, her mind completed, but her voice failed.

"I just don't understand," Will said. "You stay out
here alone when you could easily find someone to—"
he purposely played out the pause "—date." He braced
one of his arms on the back of the seat as if they had the
rest of the evening to continue the discussion, and asked
the question that had been bugging him for days. "How
long are you going to give him?"

"Who?"

Carolina looked ready to throttle him, Will decided,
but at least she was still in the conversation. Maybe if
he got her mad enough she'd really talk. If only to shut
him up. He braced himself. "Your ex-husband."

She stared at him in silence, as if she might be counting to ten. When she spoke, her words came out in the
calming voice of an orderly assigned to deal with the
resident moron. "I don't have any idea what my brother
told you, but—"

"He told me you were still in love with . . . Paul." He
couldn't resist putting an unpleasant spin on the man's
name. Ex-husbands were fair game, as far as he was
concerned. "A woman as attractive as you are shouldn't
have to—"

"Look." Light flooded the interior of the truck as
Carolina opened the door. She slid from the truck and
pinned him with a glacial stare. "My brother is an idiot
sometimes. And I hired you to build my house, not to
straighten out my love life. Go back to the bar and take
care of your own." After the door slammed, she added,
"Thanks for the beer."

As Will watched Carolina stomp up the stairs to the
front door of the cabin, he briefly wondered if she in-

tended to lock him out. He'd made her mad, all right, when all he'd really wanted to do was get her to relax and have a good time. Will shook his head. If he lived to be a hundred he'd still never understand women who nursed a torch for a man who'd deserted them, or worse.

For some reason he'd thought Carolina would be different. That maybe she hadn't run into the right man yet. Hell, at this rate, if she purposely stayed isolated twenty miles out of town, the only man she was likely to run into in the near future was him, and he—

He'd promised Brad . . . to help Carolina.

The memory of holding her in his arms as he'd carried her up the stairs, then as they'd danced, rolled over him. She'd let him get that close, she must trust him a little.

Wouldn't Brad be happier if Carolina was really over her divorce? If she'd actually let another man into her life even on a short-term basis?

Will knew how to be the available male. He'd learned that lesson in spades from Diane. She'd spun his head full of you're-the-best-thing-that's-ever-happened-to-me promises. He'd kept her hot and happy, until her ex-husband walked through the door and asked her to come back to him. Only this time, with Carolina, there would be no love involved, no attachment. He would get her over her divorce and then they could both move on.

First he had to climb out of the hole he'd dug for himself by saying too much too soon. He was definitely in the red as far as Carolina was concerned. Will smiled ruefully and opened the door of the truck. If she hadn't locked him out, that would be a start.

WILL BRACED THE BOTTOM of the timber with his boot as Mike swung it into place with the block and tackle. This was the kind of work he loved, fitting and shaping each timber together into a framework that would last a hundred years. Mary mortise and Tommy tenon, male- into female-beam sex.

Out of the corner of his vision, he could see Carolina walking down the trail toward them. She stopped at the edge of the site. He was still letting the dust settle from their confrontation a week before. She'd been cool toward him since then.

He smiled at Mike. "Haven't you got the temporary in yet? You're getting slow in your old age."

"Is that so?" Mike grunted as he pushed, trying to get the peg holes aligned. "You know I could take a lunch break and leave you standing there holding this thing up."

Will laughed but withheld his next comment.

"Knock it out a little on the bottom—away from me," Mike instructed.

Will took up the five-pound sledge at his feet and swung it against the weight of the beam. On the second swing, the brace Mike was holding shifted and fell into place. He shoved the temporary through the hole. "That's got it," he said, brushing off his hands.

Will released his hold on the heavy beam. He could feel Carolina's gaze on him, but he resisted the urge to pivot toward her. He pulled on his shirt as he moved to meet her at the ramp that ran from ground level to floor level. He'd been very careful for the past six days and five nights. He wasn't going to push her any further until they were back on friendly terms.

"I brought you guys some cold water and sodas," she said as she offered him a small cooler. She held a camera in her other hand. "I thought I'd take some photos of this stage."

Will rummaged around in the cooler and pulled out a bottle of water. He tossed it to Mike and found another one for himself. "This is the time to get a good look at the frame. After the house is finished, only about a quarter of the major wood joinery will be visible on the inside."

"Well, I'll have pictures." She smiled, but without much humor.

Will took several swallows of water from the bottle then tugged his bandanna from his back pocket and wet it. He ran the cool cloth over his forehead and along the back of his neck. When he looked up again, he noticed that Carolina's forced smile had disappeared. "Thanks," he said. "Between the dust and the low humidity I feel like I've been freeze-dried."

Carolina felt like kicking herself for being there. She'd convinced herself that watching every stage of the framing was unnecessary. But each day, for one reason or another, she'd come back. And each day she'd found herself paying more attention to Will than observing the art of heavy-timber building. For a second, she could almost hear Sue Ann's knowing laughter.

As Will took another drink from the bottle of water, condensation dripped onto his chest and the open edge of his shirt. When he pushed the bandanna across his skin to soak up the drops, Carolina turned and walked away, feeling like a pervert. Get it over with, she fumed to herself. Take the blasted pictures and leave!

Fang chose that moment to come bounding up the ramp with a two-foot-long pine branch. He dropped it at her feet and gazed up expectantly. Out of reflex, she bent over and picked it up.

"Now you've done it," Will said.

Carolina swiveled in his direction. He was tying the wet bandanna around his forehead. "Done what?" she asked.

"If you pick up the stick, that means you want to play. He's been after me all morning."

Carolina offered the stick to Will. He grinned and raised a hand in refusal. "You picked it up. You'll have to figure out how to get rid of him. He doesn't take no for an answer."

Carolina faced Fang and had to smile. He watched her with the posture and alertness of the Queen's guard at Buckingham Palace. Balanced on the pads of his feet, only one thing in the universe seemed to matter to him—the stick. Carolina flung it as hard as she could.

Will moved up behind her as Fang sprinted through the building site in pursuit. "Better watch out." Will's words sounded amused and intimate. "You might get to like him."

A warm current surged through Carolina. She glanced over her shoulder.

"I do like him," she said, unable to resist the warmth. The reflection of the trees around them seemed to intensify the color of Will's green eyes as he held her gaze.

"You could have fooled me."

The conversation had subtly changed character. Carolina wasn't sure they were still discussing the dog. "I just don't want to get too attached—"

"Hey, Will? Are you quitting for the day, or can you give me a hand here?" Mike's words coincided with Fang's return. "I need the number four brace."

"I'm on it," Will answered, but he didn't move. He looked like he had something else to say. But after a moment, with one quick pat on the dog's head, he turned and walked away.

Carolina tried her best not to stare when he shrugged out of his shirt and hung it on one of the pegs sticking from a beam. She should be used to this by now. She should be immune to his broad back and to his blatant physical appeal. But she wasn't. He'd put his shirt on when she showed up. Was it a courtesy, or protection from her mesmerized gaze? She trained her eyes on Mike and forced a smile. "Sorry, I didn't mean to interrupt."

Mike wiped a sleeve over his damp forehead and grinned. "Don't worry about it. If I didn't give him a hard time, he wouldn't know how to act."

With Fang trailing her, she moved a safe distance from the block and tackle. When she reached the bottom of the ramp, she took the stick from Fang and threw it again. While the dog was occupied, she snapped a few pictures.

The house, her house, was becoming a reality right before her eyes, and she already loved it. Will and Mike planed and fitted each beam with as much care and skill as she put into any of the unique pieces of her jewelry. The idea of building the house had been self-defense. A way to heal her life with something she could control. The reality was much, much better than she'd hoped. How often did you see the face or know the name of the person who built your home? Or even its furnishings? The house was unique, one of a kind, like the man building it, and Carolina knew she would never forget this process. That she would never look at or live one day her new home without thinking of Will, and the care he had put into it.

Fang returned after a longer search than usual. Carolina glanced down as she automatically reached for the stick. She quickly withdrew her hand.

"Yuck!" She backed away from the dog.

"What is it?" Will called.

"He brought me a dead lizard," she answered as she put her hand in her pocket, safely away from Fang's present. The animal had obviously had been dead for a while; it was stiff. Undaunted, Fang dropped it at her feet.

Both Mike and Will laughed. Still smiling, Will shook his head as he kicked the bottom of the next timber. "You're in trouble now. It must be love."

"Great." Carolina edged away from the dog and moved toward the trail. "I think I'll pass on lizard tossing, and get back to work."

"I'M NOT SURE you understand how much this house means to me," Carolina said. She and Will were once again sitting on the porch after dinner, this time in facing chairs. The growing shadows under the trees and the night sounds of crickets announced the shift from day into twilight. "Watching you and Mike work today really brought it home to me." She turned to face him. For some reason, the truth seemed a little easier to tell tonight. What difference would it make if he knew? "It started out as my diversion. A way to get past the divorce." She had no husband or family, but she would have a home. "Dreaming about it and planning it gave me back a future." She waited for Will to pounce on that one.

He didn't. "And?"

Carolina swallowed, choking a little on the next nugget of truth. "I wasn't sure how someone like you, who lives like a gypsy and doesn't seem to want to own anything, could possibly build the house of my dreams."

Will simply stared at her.

She tried to smile. "I have to tell you, though. After seeing you work, I think maybe you do understand. Or at least you love what you do, and it shows."

"Thank you . . . I think," Will said without smiling. A few long moments of silence spun out between them in the darkening twilight. Carolina felt like squirming.

"You're wrong about me not wanting to own anything," he said finally. "As a matter of fact, I intend to build this house—the one I'm building for you—for myself someday."

"When you settle down." Carolina couldn't keep the skepticism out of her voice. Some men never settled down, even when they married.

"Yeah. Well, you're right about that one. I'm not sure when that'll be. I tried it once," Will said, "but it didn't take." Carolina glanced at him, but his eyes were trained on the trees, on the sky or on the past. "I almost got married and did the whole family thing."

"What happened?"

"It didn't work out."

She would have called Will on the cliché if his voice hadn't sounded so somber. "Why not?" He'd brought it up, but suddenly she had to know.

"She, uh . . ." He shifted in the chair, stretching his long legs and crossing them at the ankles. "The woman I— Diane was separated from her husband. We were planning to get married when the divorce was final."

Carolina knew how it felt to be on the other end of that scenario, but she withheld judgment. "And?"

Will's eyes met hers. "A week before the final papers were supposed to be signed, she decided she wanted to go back to him."

The look on Will's face made Carolina's throat ache, and she felt a sharp twist of anger toward the woman who had hurt him. She had no idea what to say, so she blundered on. "Why?"

Will shrugged and withdrew his gaze. When he spoke, his voice had an angry edge to it. "Beats the hell out of me. I thought things were good, that we—"

"Maybe she was scared."

"Of me?" he said, anger changing to incredulous surprise.

"No," Carolina added quickly. "Afraid of change, of making an irrevocable decision or mistake. Believe me, it's a scary place to be." Why was she making excuses for a woman who had supposedly done the right thing and gone back to her husband? She'd never even considered, before now, that every heart involved in a triangle could get broken.

"Yeah, well. I thought the two of us were making a decision together, but as it turned out, I wasn't included." He was quiet again for a short span. "I heard later that they finally did get divorced. But I wasn't going to ante into that game again. It worked out for the best anyway. I don't think I would have been happy staying in one place, with one woman."

"At least you're honest about it." Carolina sighed. "In my experience, men want it all. They want to follow their careers and take their families with them. They want one woman at home, and the freedom to have any of the others that cross their path." Carolina winced at the underlying anger in her comment. She was angry at Paul because he'd made her feel like a failure. And she didn't like it, or deserve it. Loving someone only set you up to lose. First your heart, then your trust, then your future.

"Sounds like your ex-husband is a great guy."

Feeling contrite and confused by her anger, Carolina amended her caustic words. "He wasn't so bad," she admitted. "He worked hard. He wasn't abusive or crazy." Now it was her turn to stare into the unblinking truth of the past. "He just wasn't honest with himself, or with me."

"That's a tough one, the honesty thing. I think a lot of men decide there are things a woman doesn't need to know about them. So they say what they think the woman wants to hear. Having been on the shi—" he stopped "—uh, on the nasty end of that stick, I'd rather get or give the bad news up front."

The darkness around them was almost complete. Carolina could barely see Will's features. It made it easier to talk. "Well, here's some honesty for you. You're doing a great job on the house and I appreciate it. And I'm sorry I doubted you."

A low laugh drifted across the darkness. "Well, that sounded painful. But I'll take any compliment I can get."

Carolina breathed a sigh of relief. He'd let her off easier and with more grace than she'd expected.

"So what are your plans after this job? Do you have something else lined up?" she asked. It seemed to take a long time for him to answer what Carolina had assumed was a simple question.

"My plan for this year was to be in Japan, but that's another one of those things that didn't work out." He didn't sound angry, only puzzled. "Don't get me wrong," he continued. "I'm happy to be here, working on your house. But I apprenticed in Germany, and although they have the technical side of joinery down to a science, the Japanese are artists." She sensed more than saw him look in her direction. "You should be able to appreciate that.

"Anyway—" his voice betrayed his disappointment "—what seemed like the perfect opportunity to work with the Japanese, and to help hand-build something with meaning, something sacred, like the temple, fizzled out."

Carolina struggled for hopeful words. She knew how it felt to watch plans and dreams fall through or be put off time after time. Year after year. And she could understand the call of artistry. Of setting out to build something unique, that would last, for reasons other than money.

"It'll happen," she said. "You'll go." She withheld the comment that he had plenty of time. Sometimes waiting could be harder than failing. "Excuse me for sounding selfish, but I'm glad you're in Prescott, Arizona—at least for the next few months."

"Glad enough to make more of those blueberry muffins I had when I first got here?"

Carolina laughed. She pushed out of her chair to go inside. "It's a deal, timber man."

THE FRAME WAS UP. Will walked around the site from beam to beam, pushing and pulling, checking the pegs and the joinery. Everything had to be right. He wanted this to be the tightest and truest frame he and Mike had ever put together.

He wanted Carolina to love this house.

She'd come out to the site once a day to talk, to see the progress and to take pictures. He liked that. He enjoyed the sensation of looking up and finding her gaze on him. Today she'd be surprised. The frame was finished. He and Mike were going into town later to celebrate, and he wanted Carolina along. He had to figure out the right way to ask her to go. He wanted to dance with her again, to hold her in his arms and show her that there were other men in the world besides her ex-husband. He heard Mike speaking to someone and turned just as Carolina raised the camera to her eye.

Carolina snapped the picture of the finished frame, then realized that most of the photos she'd taken had Will in them. It wasn't only the process of building that she wanted to remember, it was the man who had done the work. And what was wrong with that? she argued with herself. What was wrong with remembering someone who'd done something extraordinary for her? He was building her home and in the process he had helped her look forward to the future instead of staring at the pain of the past.

"This is the part I like the best," Will said as he jumped down from the foundation to ground level. He walked toward her with a satisfied, thousand-watt smile that nearly melted her shoes. "What do you think?"

Carolina couldn't think, she could only grin at him. She felt as though she and Will had accomplished something together—like proud parents. He moved next to her and turned toward the frame.

"You'll never see it like this again. This is the heart of the house. As soon as the walls are framed in, it'll be hidden. You did a great job, man," he said as he turned to Mike and offered his hand for a high five.

"I did, didn't I?" Mike laughed before returning the slap. "Listen, I'm going back to get cleaned up and then

I'll meet you later, right?" His question seemed to include Carolina, and although she didn't know what he was talking about, she smiled.

With a wave, Mike picked up his tool bag, dropped it into the trunk of his borrowed car and backed out of the drive, leaving Carolina alone with Will and her unfinished house.

"It's beautiful," Carolina managed as silence surrounded them once more. "It's a shame to cover the timbers up. At this stage, the frame looks like a sculpture."

"It would be pretty difficult to live in it like it is, since only the toolroom is covered," Will teased. "So, I guess I'll have to get someone to build you a few walls and a complete roof."

"Gee, thanks," Carolina said, heavy on the sarcasm.

Will laughed and pulled the camera out of her hand. "Go stand over there and let me take a picture of you—" his voice took on the tone of a TV salesman "—and your custom-built, heavy-timber frame."

Carolina's hand automatically went to her hair. The braid was always coming loose.

"You look fine," Will said, reading the gesture. "Here." He led her to the elevated foundation, set the camera on the top of it and spanned her waist with his large hands.

He stepped close, and Carolina's breath seemed to desert her completely. In one easy motion he lifted her to sit on the foundation. Suddenly, she was on the same level with his amazing green eyes, and pictures were the furthest thing from her thoughts.

He didn't step back as she expected. His hands fell away from her waist to rest on the wood at either side of her hips. Although he wasn't touching her, he stood there, intimately situated between her thighs. As he scanned her features, a blush of embarrassment moved under the skin of her face and an answering rush of heat flared downward to her toes. She felt surrounded . . . and revealed. She couldn't speak or look away as she watched his gaze lower to her mouth. God, what was she supposed to do? He looked like he was going to kiss her.

The sound of a car rumbling down the road behind him snagged Will's attention. He was close enough to claim the kiss he'd been contemplating, but . . . He frowned and turned to face the intruder. If Mike had come back for some stupid reason, he was going to kill him.

It was a white pickup truck—not Mike. Fang sprinted alongside the truck, which was emblazoned with the words Kirkland Fencing. Will backed away as Carolina slid from her elevated seat to stand on the ground.

"How's it going?" the man called as he slammed the door of his truck. He wore a baseball cap, with Kirkland Fencing embroidered across the front, over dark hair that had a sprinkling of gray interspersed at his temples. Will watched him walk toward them with relative equanimity, figuring he was one of the suppliers from town. Fang dogged the man's heels, but he ignored him.

"Hi," Carolina called as he approached. The moment she stepped forward to greet him, Will realized where he'd seen the man before. This was the guy who had tried to hit on her when they were in the Square Peg Tavern. The intense urge to send him packing roared through Will.

"Jimmy Kirkland, this is Will Case. He's building my house," Carolina said. Will stood silent, watching her, wondering how glad she was to see Jimmy Kirkland again. He frowned.

Jimmy extended his hand. After a brief handshake, Will casually sized him up in case sending him packing became an option. He almost smiled at the thought, but he didn't want Jimmy to consider him friendly.

"You've gotten a lot of work done out here," Jimmy said, keeping his eyes on Carolina.

"Yes, we—"

"We have a ways to go yet." Will purposely interrupted. He wasn't going to make it easy for the guy. Jimmy glanced in Will's direction as if he'd forgotten his presence, then returned his concentration to Carolina.

"What gave you the idea to build a wild house like this one?"

"Nothing wild about it," Will answered in a falsely congenial voice. The kind of voice he usually used right before he told someone to kiss his— "It's one of the oldest forms of building construction known."

Carolina frowned in his direction. Will almost winced.

No doubt she was annoyed and probably on the verge of demanding to know what was going on. She gave him one more hard look before defending her own decision by saying, "I like the plan."

Jimmy stepped past her to gaze at the frame. "Well, it looks solid enough, but I bet it cost you a fortune to do it that way."

Now Kirkland was worried about her money. It was all Will could do not to grab him by his collar and the seat of his pants and—

"It's what I wanted," Carolina said to his back. She sounded a little irritated with him, as well.

"And it didn't cost a fortune," Will added for good measure.

Jimmy pivoted to face them and shrugged. He glanced at Will again, but addressed Carolina. "Well, I came out to talk about building you a fence."

Without even stopping to wonder, Will decided he'd had enough of this guy. He stood with his arms crossed, glowering toward Jimmy with what could be mildly labeled as unfriendly intentions. "She doesn't need a fence."

Jimmy pushed his cap back on his head, and for a moment Will had the hope that he would just go for it. Instead, he casually raised a hand in Fang's direction. "I saw that dog out on the main road when I came in."

"She doesn't need a fence," Will repeated. "He's my dog and I—"

"Will—" Carolina's voice was tight with anger. She shifted her hands to her hips and stopped him with one of those enough-is-enough stares. Will stared back at her, wondering how far he could push it. Why didn't she just tell this butthead to get lost? Why couldn't *he* let it go? That sent a jolt through him. He'd wanted her to find another man, to get over her divorce. Didn't he? If this was the man for the job . . .

Without a word, Will turned and walked away. He forced his mind from the uncomfortable image of this man touching Carolina and centered his thoughts on collecting the tools scattered around the site.

"I'm sorry," Carolina said to Jimmy as her gaze followed Will's unhurried movements. She didn't want a fence, but she didn't want to discuss it now. "I—I'll have to talk to you about it another time."

Jimmy removed his hat and ran one hand through his hair before replacing it. A gesture that looked nervous and relieved at the same time. "Yeah. You call me when you've got some time to talk." With that, he walked toward his truck, got in, revved the engine and drove off.

"What was that about?" Carolina asked Will, barely able to resist the impulse to shout at him.

He didn't look at her. Instead, he bent down to pick up one of the sledges. "What was what about?" He returned the question innocently. Before Carolina knew it, she had grasped the solid weight of his arm and forced him to look at her.

"That whole business about the fence." She drew her hand away and straightened her spine. "The sudden need you have to answer questions for me."

"I didn't like the guy." He started to turn away.

Carolina yanked his arm again. "This isn't about him. This is about me. Why do you think you have the right to step in and decide what questions I should answer, or what friends I should—"

"You know something? You're right." Will's voice had risen in tone. He dropped the hammer he'd been holding and bracketed her shoulders with his hands. "This is about you."

Before Carolina could react, Will pressed her backward until she was pinned against the immovable weight of one of the beams. Fang circled them in playful confusion and started barking.

"Beat it, Fang!" Will ordered, never taking his gaze from Carolina's face. "You know what that guy wants, and it has nothing to do with building fences," he said. He was so close to her, she could feel his breath rush out along with his words. "If you need a man, at least choose one with a little more going for him than chain link."

Angry words collided together in Carolina's brain scrambling for release, but she was so furious she couldn't speak. How dare he criticize anything about her life? Especially her sex life? *If you need a man...* She gritted her teeth. Even if he was right, even if she did need a man, even if she wanted *him*—it was none of his business!

She lifted her chin, ignored the strong fingers wrapped around her upper arms and found her best condescending, big-sister voice. "You sound like Brad." She looked into his eyes, communicating her aggravation, her age advantage—anything that would set him back on his heels. "Does everything for guys your age have to do with sex?"

That stopped him. For a microsecond she held the advantage. If he would just let her go for a moment... Suddenly his hands relaxed, but he didn't let go. His long fingers readjusted on her arms, from holding to touching. Heat seemed to gather under his palms, and Carolina swallowed against this new, less angry but more physical threat to her sanity.

"Well, if you weren't Brad's sister, we wouldn't even be having this...disagreement." The low, suggestive tone of his voice sent a shiver of apprehension through Carolina. And a shimmering of pleasure. His expression softened, his green eyes communicated heat and promise.

He had changed right in front of her eyes, his anger gone or well hidden. She held onto hers like a shield. "Oh, really? Why? Because I'd be in your bed?" She purposely made the idea sound ludicrous. She had to convince him, to convince herself that it would be crazy to even consider such a thing.

His fingers shifted over the fabric of her sleeves, slowly, slightly. Enough to make Carolina realize her sarcasm hadn't affected him. And enough for her to recognize that she was up to her neck and surrounded by about two hundred and twenty pounds of pure male hormones.

"No," he said finally, with a twist of a smile that was slow and hot. "Because I'd be in yours."

Then his lips were on hers.

Carolina managed to make a sound, although even she wasn't sure whether it was in protest or surrender. He possessed her mouth firmly, as if to prevent any chance she might have used to speak or to pull away. When his tongue stroked the seam of her lips, demanding entry, the memory of weeks of tension urged her to open, to participate. She wanted to be kissed, to taste him. His tongue grazed hers, coaxing, directing. A shudder ran through her, heat and need exploding. Just a kiss and then she would stop him, her mind bargained.

But her hard-earned caution interrupted, clanging in warning that in one more moment she would be unable to stop him. Not because he was bigger or stronger, but because she wouldn't want to stop him. And she had learned that wanting too much only led to pain.

She pushed at his chest and twisted away from the wet heat of his mouth.

"Don't!"

The silence that followed hummed in Carolina's ears as she stared at him. Will looked stunned, and she felt like crying.

Anger and sadness and yearning swamped her. Anger that she couldn't hide from the truth for just a little while, long enough to share something with Will. And sadness because she wished she could. No, she wouldn't want to be twenty something again. Not unless she knew everything she knew now. So that when he left it wouldn't hurt so much.

"You don't understand. I can't play games, I can't just—"

"I'm not playing a game," he said, and leaned close again.

She pushed harder against his chest. "Don't make me choose between you or the house, Will."

He stopped abruptly, as though he'd bumped into the invisible barrier of her words, her choices.

"Please . . ." The itch of tears clogged her throat. She had to get out of there.

Will didn't try to stop her. He was struggling with his own reactions. He'd kissed Carolina whether she'd wanted him to or not. He hadn't wanted to surprise her, or to punish her, or even to impress her. He'd kissed her because, when he was face-to-face with her, tasting her mouth had become the most vital concern in his mind, the most out-of-control need of his body. He ran a hand over his face. He'd never had to force a woman to do anything in his life.

He'd wanted to punch the fence man. What was happening to him? How had he gotten so involved with Carolina's protection . . . and needs? It really was none of his business. So why had the idea of her with Kirkland hit such a gut-wrenching nerve? The answer rearended the question. Because he wanted to be the one to make her forget about the past, about her ex-husband.

He'd wanted to give her a slow, tongue-teasing kiss that would have explained everything. A kiss that would have proved what she needed and what he could give, but she'd pulled away.

He wanted her . . . bad. For her own good, and his. But instead of giving him welcome, or even warmth, she'd made him feel like an adolescent with a crush on the baby-sitter. He knew he was treading on hazardous ground. She was the boss here and he merely an employee. She was well within her rights to call the law and have him thrown off the property.

Why was he doing this? He'd never had to linger where he wasn't wanted. Finding a woman had never been a problem. He needed to let Carolina go. If she was still mad at her ex-husband, then maybe no other man had a chance. Anger meant feelings, and feelings could sometimes get twisted around into love. He knew from past experience that a woman might say she's angry, but with the right persuasion she'd fall back into the man's arms.

He tossed the last of the tools into the toolroom and shut the door. He'd been trying to be the hero, to fix the problem he recognized. If Carolina didn't want him, then there were plenty of other faces who would return his smile, his interest. But, for a few seconds, as he'd stared into Carolina's amber eyes, he'd thought he'd seen a reflection of his need. No. He pushed the image away.

He was going out tonight to find a woman. One who wasn't overly fond of the word no. That way at least half of the problem between him and Carolina would be solved. One of them would feel better.

Carolina was on the phone when he walked through the door of the cabin a few minutes later. She glanced toward him nervously and said into the phone, "Okay. No, don't come here."

Will stopped in his tracks. He felt like he'd been punched. Who was she talking to? Kirkland? Her gaze slipped away from his. "I'll meet you there at seven. Bye."

She hung up the phone, and without a word of explanation to him headed for the kitchen.

Stay away from her, Will, his mind ordered. *Don't get crazy.* He turned in the opposite direction and took the stairs two at a time. He had to get out of there for a while, and fast. He snatched up some clean jeans in his room and stomped down the stairs to take a shower.

Carolina felt like screaming. She had to get away from Will. She'd tried to convince herself that the friction between them was just cabin fever. That they'd simply been cooped up together in close quarters for too long. But she knew it was more than that—more than hormones. It was getting crazy. She could barely meet his eyes because each look made her feel dazed and desperate. Out of control.

She rattled around in a cupboard looking for a pot. She'd heat up something for his dinner, then meet Sue Ann. She didn't know what else to do. She was afraid. If he pressed the issue—if he kissed her again or even pulled her close—she wouldn't be able to say no. She could still taste his mouth on hers, feel the heat. She had to get out of the house, out of his vicinity until she could bolster her defenses.

Sue Ann would be no help at all. She could almost hear the words. "So what's wrong with having a little fling with a good-looking guy? You're divorced, not dead."

I'll tell you what's wrong, she fumed in silent answer. The only thing going for her and Will was the fact that one of them happened to be male and the other female. Everything else was wrong. He was too young. She was too cynical. He was too physically attractive. She was too self-conscious. He was too young! He belonged with a younger woman. He might be interested in making a conquest, or worse, he might feel sorry for her because she was alone. But she wasn't going to blithely fall into his arms and imagine it would make either of them happy. Or imagine he would stay.

She twisted her hands as she waited for the water to boil before adding rice. She was a thirty-six-year-old, reasonably attractive woman, but she would never be twenty-nine again. She wasn't going to pretend that time had not changed her body, or her attitude toward men.

But he did make her want. For the first time in a long time, she physically wanted a man. The memory of feeling surrounded by him, of his mouth coaxing hers, sent an echo of longing through her. She wished she had the nerve to accept what he was offering. She deserved some happiness, and he was just offering a little friendly sex. What was wrong with that?

Everything. Carolina sighed. She didn't know how to have friendly sex, and then say goodbye. Especially with Will. He was already too important to her security, her house. She couldn't let him get too important to her heart.

And he was her brother's friend. The fact that she couldn't have him rankled. Nevertheless, he had proved Sue Ann's point—she wasn't dead yet.

Carolina heard the shower shut off as she made her way upstairs to her room. Will would have to eat dinner alone. She was going to get cleaned up and meet Sue Ann. That should give them both time to get back to normal.

Carolina heard the shower shut off as she made her
way upstairs to her room. Well-would have to cut dinner short. She was going to get dressed up and meet Sue
Ann. That would give the neighbors time to get back to

6

"SO, WHICH MOVIE do you want to see?"

Carolina drew her gaze away from the flashing neon
sign on the front of a store. She had met Sue Ann in the
parking lot of a small shopping center, and now they
were both seated in Sue Ann's four-wheel-drive truck.
Glancing toward the newspaper that was open to the
movie section, Carolina shrugged. "You choose."

Sue Ann lost interest in the paper. "What's the matter?"

"Nothing," Carolina lied, thinking of the expression
on Will's face earlier when she had jerked away from
his kiss. Everything was the matter. By the time she'd
taken a shower and gotten herself dressed and under
control, he'd been gone. Where was he now?

"Come on, Caro. I know you better than that. What
is it? Have you heard from Paul?"

Carolina returned her attention to her friend. "No,
it isn't Paul." *For once*, her mind added. She sighed.
"I'm having a little problem with Will."

"What kind of problem?"

"I— He—"

"Come on, spit it out," Sue Ann coaxed.

"He kissed me." Carolina felt the movement of
warmth upward from her neck to her cheeks, then
along the back of her neck. The aftereffects still lin-
gered.

"Really?" She could tell she had Sue Ann's complete and undivided attention. "And?"

"And I liked it," Carolina admitted in a rush. *Liked?* Part of her wanted to laugh hysterically at such a luke-warm description, but the rest of her was too confused and too worried.

"Well—"

"I know what you're going to say—" she spoke quickly to forestall her friend "—that I should go for it. And I have to admit that I'm tempted. But—"

"Wait a minute," Sue Ann interrupted. "Granted, I would like to see you with some male companionship, but I haven't even met the guy. What is it about him that has you so upset?"

Carolina slumped against the seat and stared out the front window. "He's twenty-nine years old. He's Brad's best friend, for God's sake. Can you picture me getting involved with someone like my brother? You've met Brad. You've seen how he acts."

"Is kissing Will like kissing your brother? Is that the problem?"

Carolina's face grew even hotter. "No, I don't mean . . . He's not like my brother. He's—"

"I don't see the big dilemma here," Sue Ann pushed on. "If he's not like your brother and you enjoy kissing him—"

"He's the first man I have been attracted to since Paul," Carolina admitted, knowing attraction was way too mild a term for what she felt for Will. She looked at her hands folded in her lap. "But it's all wrong. He's been very nice but . . ."

"What are you afraid of?"

A sudden bleak picture entered Carolina's mind. She sighed and glanced up. "I think he just feels sorry for me. He's doing me a favor. He's always saying I shouldn't be alone, that I should be dating someone."

"And he wants to be that someone."

Carolina managed a short, humorless laugh. "We would hardly have to date. We're living in the same house."

"I think you should take him up on the offer."

"I knew you would," Carolina said without missing a beat. "But what about my house?" *What about my heart?* she added silently. The thought of undressing in front of Will, of allowing him to see and explore all her imperfections, chased any idea of passion out of her head. She'd been rejected by Paul because she didn't live up to his standard. How could she set herself up to be rejected again, and by Will? "I need Will to build my house more than I need him to . . . date." She couldn't even say it without graphic images of her and Will together springing to mind. "If our personal relationship somehow ends up in ruins, how will we live and work together?"

Sue Ann watched her for a long moment. "I see your point, but I know you. And I know there's more to it than that."

"You haven't seen him. You haven't seen how other women notice him." The next words tasted bitter in her mouth. "You know, I never even thought about my age until Paul and I split up. Divorce has a way of making you realize how much of your life has gone by." *Especially when your husband left you for a younger woman.* Carolina closed her eyes for a few seconds. "What could a young, attractive guy like Will possibly want from me?"

Sue Ann tugged at her arm. "Obviously, he wants to be more than friends. Carolina, you're in great shape.

You've got a good body and incredible eyes that I would kill to have. You're smart, successful . . ." When she got no response, Sue Ann grumbled, "Speaking of killing . . . I would love to take out a contract on Paul—in retribution for the murder of your self-esteem." She sounded truly incensed, and it made Carolina smile.

"I've thought about it," Carolina quipped and smiled at her friend. "But life in prison is a little too settled for me. Besides, it's my problem, not Paul's."

"That's debatable. You know, sooner or later you're going to have to face this fear of starting over. If you take a chance with Will, what's the worst that could happen?"

"He'll leave me."

Sue Ann looked surprised. "How do you know you'll want him to stay? Are you going to demand a guarantee before you even decide to get involved?"

Now it was Carolina's turn to be surprised. She hadn't considered the fact that she wasn't emotionally involved with Will—only physically attracted. He wasn't Paul, someone she had loved and trusted and built a life with.

"There's nothing wrong with asking for what you want. If you want Will and if you feel strong enough emotionally to take a chance, go for it."

Was she emotionally strong enough? Carolina wondered. She knew Will would leave when the house was finished. She *knew* it—leaving was a way of life for him. Maybe Sue Ann was right. Maybe the time had come to face her fear.

"So? I want to know what you're going to do."

Carolina reached across the console and dragged the newspaper closer. "Right now? I'm going to pick a movie with no sex and a lot of violence."

WILL CHALKED the end of his cue and scanned the table for his next shot. It had been awhile since he'd played pool on a regular basis so he was a little rusty. He glanced at Mike, who was grinning at him from the opposite side of the table, and decided to try a difficult cushion shot. As he bent over to line up the cue ball, a body brushed against him.

"Excuse me," a woman's voice apologized.

Will arched a look over his shoulder and was awarded with a smile. Couldn't be more than twenty-one, he decided, but she had a grown-up look in her eyes.

He nodded, then made the shot. Mike sauntered around the table and watched the woman walk away. "What happened to the boss lady tonight? Not in the mood to celebrate?"

The memory of Carolina's eyes filling with tears after he had tried to kiss her made Will grit his teeth. "No," he said finally and turned to the table to line up his next shot. He wanted to concentrate on the angles and trajectories of playing pool—and on the distinct possibility of getting drunk. He didn't want to think about Carolina. "Catch the waitress and order me a tequila shooter," he said as he struck the ball with the cue.

They gave up on pool after three more games. Will had redeemed his reputation by winning three out of five. The bar was getting crowded and the band was into the second set of the evening but he hadn't even managed to feel better, much less get a buzz. With his back propped against the bar, Will watched the dancers. His eyes stopped on the woman who had brushed against him earlier. She and two of her friends were bumping and grinding their way through one of those elaborate line dances. And she was smiling again, di-

rectly at him. He knew he should smile back. That's
why he'd come here in the first place. To find a woman.
But all he could think about was Carolina. What was
she doing? Was she thinking about him? Or was she
with Jimmy Kirkland?

The song ended. As the dancers left the floor Will
turned to order another shot of tequila. When he turned
around, the woman was standing at his elbow.

"Hi," she said, before leaning against the bar next to
him. A sweet, flowery cloud of perfume drifted around
him.

"Hi," he returned. A little too much makeup, but at
least she didn't have a hundred pounds of stiff hair.

"Want to dance?" she asked.

Why the hell not? Will gave Mike a look that warned
him not to say a word as the woman took his arm and
pulled him toward the dance floor.

They danced to three or four songs, the last of which
was a slow song. As Will pulled the woman closer, the
memory of dancing with Carolina robbed him of any
enjoyment. He suddenly knew he couldn't—that he
needed a woman, but not the one who was currently in
his arms. He turned his face away from her hair and
tried to remember Carolina's smell, the feel of her
breasts pressed against his chest. It made him want to
swear.

As the last few notes of the music played out, Will
excused himself and went to find Mike. He glanced at
the clock behind the bar. It was only ten-thirty. He
couldn't go back to the cabin yet. And he wasn't drunk.
He looked toward the front entrance of the bar and
wished for what he really wanted. He wished that Carolina would walk through the door.

He pulled his mind away from that fantasy, and he and Mike fell into a discussion of Mike's impending trip home. The next time he looked at the clock, it was five till eleven. Peripherally, Will saw the woman he had been dancing with walking his way. *Damn.* He shifted his gaze to the front door again and frowned.

AFTER A FINAL NUDGE from Sue Ann, Carolina pushed open the door of the Square Peg Tavern and stepped inside. She couldn't believe she'd let Sue Ann talk her into doing this. What would she say to Will? She knew he'd be here, unless he'd found other, more interesting places to go. That thought made her throat tighten.

The tavern was dark and smoky and loud. With Sue Ann at her back, she edged her way past the knot of people standing near the pool tables. Clear of the crowd, she let her eyes travel the length of the bar until she saw Mike and then Will. He was looking directly at her with a scowl on his face. He looked surprised and angry and lethal. A shiver of pure animal awareness traveled from Carolina's hair to her toenails. Fear followed. Could she go through with this? She tried to conjure up a smile but before she could manage, a woman insinuated herself next to Will and slid her arm through his. A young woman with dark hair.

Carolina stopped in her tracks, and her attempted smile died. She felt like she'd been kicked by a horse. What kind of self-delusion had made her imagine, even for a moment, that she could compete with younger women for Will's attention? She turned to Sue Ann, nearly choking on the smoke in the air and the pain in her chest. "Let's get out of here."

Sue Ann's eyes were on the crowd. "We haven't even looked yet. I want to meet him."

Unwillingly, Carolina's gaze went to Will. He'd stood up, but the woman was leaning against him now. "We're leaving," Carolina said. "Right now." She took her friend's arm to steer her toward the door.

"What's wrong?" Sue Ann asked once they reached the sidewalk in front of the bar. When Carolina didn't answer but kept walking toward the parking lot, Sue Ann continued, "You saw him, didn't you? Why didn't you at least point him out?"

Carolina had the unreasonable urge to run. To get as far from this place as she could, as fast as she could. She got into Sue Ann's truck and said, "Start the engine."

"I just wanted to see what he looked like," Sue Ann complained, but did as Carolina asked.

"He was with another woman," Carolina said as Sue Ann backed out of the parking spot. "A *younger* woman!" For a heartbeat, Sue Ann hesitated. Carolina saw the front door of the bar swing open, and her heart lurched. Absurdly, she wanted it to be Will, coming after her, but she refused to look. What if he hadn't bothered? Sue Ann put the truck in gear and drove out of the lot. About five miles down the road, Carolina began to breathe again.

She could deal with this. Hadn't she known it all along? Seducing her was probably just a game to him, a challenge. Thank God she hadn't let him kiss her. Really kiss her. She would have been mortified. She would have hated herself for being such a fool—again. Anger saved her from tears. She could deal with this.

IT WAS PAST MIDNIGHT and Will had gone beyond the point of thinking. As he closed the front door of the cabin and concentrated on making it up the stairs, he kept his mind focused on what he had to do. The walls of the upstairs hallway seemed to shrink around him, and he stopped for a moment, facing the closed door to Carolina's room.

He wanted to bang on the door and wake her up. He wanted to kick off his boots and crawl into bed with her. He wanted to hold her in his arms until she didn't want to be anywhere else. He shook his head. He had to leave.

Will turned and ducked under the low doorway of his room. He switched on the light, snatched up his duffel bag and started shoving his clothes inside. He couldn't think, or wonder, or dismiss the truth anymore. He wanted Carolina in the very physical way a man wanted a woman. She didn't want him. And he couldn't remain in the same house with her without making a jackass out of himself. Why couldn't he accept the fact that she wasn't interested? Period. He gathered up his jacket and a book he'd been trying to read for two weeks and balanced them on top of the stuffed duffel. He turned to snag the pillow from his bed, since he hadn't brought one with him. When he turned again, Carolina was standing in the doorway.

She looked sleepy and worried, and all he wanted to do was step forward and pull her into his arms. He realized he had a stranglehold on the pillow. He tossed it on top of the duffel bag but kept his distance from Carolina.

"What are you doing?" Her voice was low, hesitant.

He let his eyes sweep over her. She was wearing a pair of loose sweatpants and a big T-shirt—not exactly sexy. But she could have been dressed in a burlap sack and wrapped in poison ivy and he would have still wanted to touch her. The tension between them had gotten way out of proportion in his mind, and his body was more

than willing to press the issue. It would be safer to go.
"I'm moving out."

"What?" Her eyes widened, and he felt a momentary twinge of satisfaction for scaring her. Satisfaction shifted to guilt. This wasn't her fault. It was his own damned problem. "I'm going to sleep in the toolroom at the new house from now on. I need more space." The backs of his legs were against the edge of the bed behind him. The image of simply reaching for her and tossing her across the bed seared his nonrational brain. He cleared his throat and bent to pick up his duffel and the items on top of it. "And we could both use a little more privacy."

She stood there staring at him like he'd kicked the dog or something. He needed to ask her why she'd come to the bar earlier, and why she'd left so abruptly. Was it simply because she didn't want to be in the same room with him? Well, what he didn't need was to be hit over the head by the obvious. He intended to get beyond arm's reach, or half a hallway's distance from her, then they would both be safe.

Carolina knew Will was waiting for her to get out of his way. Her heart had nearly stopped when he'd said he was leaving—and the house had been her second thought. Her first was that she'd never see him again. That shocked her more than she wanted to admit. Her concern was for her house, wasn't it? Wasn't that all she wanted from Will?

She'd been so relieved when she'd heard the truck pull up in front of the cabin. And now he was leaving. *Let him go, Carolina*, her mind reasoned. *He's made you feel alive again—happy and sad. This has gone far enough. Be thankful, and let him go.*

She stepped out of his way.

Will walked past her without another word. She heard him go down the stairs and close the front door. Looking out her bedroom window a few moments later, she could see his large silhouette by the light of the flashlight he was carrying as he walked down the trail to the new house. The shadow of a dog danced through the light.

Carolina closed her eyes and sighed. At least Fang was happy.

7

"HI, CARO. Is Will there?" Brad's voice sounded too chipper for such an early-morning call. Carolina had barely slept the night before. She wasn't in the mood for chipper.

"He's over at the new house," she answered.

"Already? It's only—" He seemed to be juggling the phone "—by my watch and with the time change, it's only seven o'clock. I thought I'd catch him before he went to work."

Carolina figured she might as well tell him the truth. "He's sleeping at the new house now," she said, trying to make it sound offhand.

A pause followed. "You didn't throw him out of your cabin, did you?"

Carolina drew in a long breath and held her temper. Why did Brad always expect her to be the bad guy? "No," she said in a rational, calm voice, determined not to let him push her buttons. "He said he needed more room, that he—"

Brad's knowing laugh interrupted her explanation. "Oh," he said. "He's found a woman."

Carolina's rational calmness fled.

"Will always finds a woman."

The memory of walking into the Square Peg Tavern the evening before and seeing a woman take Will's arm rushed into Carolina's thoughts. A young woman with dark hair and a smile. Had she been waiting for Will last night? Had he gone to another woman after he'd packed his things and walked out of her cabin?

"Listen," Brad went on, "I just wanted to tell him that I'll be out in a few weeks. The week of the twenty-fourth." When Carolina didn't answer him, he said, "Hello? You still there?"

"Y-yes," Carolina stammered. "I, uh—"

"I know you'll be going to your show in L.A., so I thought I'd spend some time with Will. He doesn't have to pick me up. I'll rent a car in Phoenix and drive."

"That's fine. I—"

The front door of the cabin swung open and Will walked in. He looked tired and...guilty. Carolina stared at him, feeling like a fist gripped her heart.

Will glanced at the phone then gestured toward the kitchen. "I was going to make some coffee. I didn't think you'd be up."

"Hang on a minute," she said to Brad. "Here." She handed Will the phone, unable to meet his gaze. "It's for you."

From the kitchen, Carolina could hear Will's low voice, but she didn't hear the words. She didn't want to know what Will had been doing.

Time to let it go, Carolina's mind whispered. She kept her attention on the efficient movements of her hands, on making coffee and arranging cups and bowls. As soon as breakfast was set out, she could escape up-stairs. She had received her answer about facing her fear the night before. She wasn't up to playing the hormone game. She didn't want to give a damn who Will was involved with. Giving in to the physical attraction between them had been a nice fantasy—for about thirty seconds. And then reality had hit. So there was no rea-

son to be upset or surprised by anything he decided to
do.

What if she had actually fallen into his arms, his
bed... and then had to watch him walk away with a
woman closer to his own age, or younger? Or had to
watch him choke on his breakfast trying to be polite to
her after deciding to move on. She'd had enough pain
from Paul's choices. She wasn't going to get involved
with Will's.

She didn't look at Will as she walked by him on her
way upstairs. The distance between them seemed to
widen with each step she took. *It's better this way,* she
decided. They were strangers, after all. And she intended to keep it that way.

CAROLINA picked up the small hammer and gently
tapped the edge of the silver framework designed to
hold a piece of polished lapis. She usually listened to
music as she worked, but today the uncommon sound
of rain pounding on the roof of her studio was her ac-
companiment. It didn't rain often in northern Arizona, but when it did, the pace was fast and furious.
Carolina's gaze drifted toward the window. She was
cozy and dry in her studio. She wondered what Will
was doing.

For the past two weeks, he'd made himself scarce
around her cabin. And she'd kept her distance from the
house site. In the mornings, she purposely waited until
after he'd had breakfast or coffee and left before she
came downstairs. In the evenings, after getting cleaned
up, he drove into town for dinner. The only time he'd
intentionally sought her out was when he'd brought
Mike over to say goodbye.

The nights were a little more difficult. Carolina sighed and picked up the stone to test the fit of the setting. The sudden emptiness of her cabin and the visions of Will with another woman had tormented her the first few nights. She glanced at the Band-Aid decorating one of her fingers like an award for lack of concentration. But she felt better now. Now that she'd gained some physical and mental distance from him.

She held up the setting and admired the multi-layered colors of azure blue and indigo frozen in the polished surface of the lapis. There was no harm in her being attracted to Will, as long as she never acted on that attraction . . . as long as he never found out.

A bump and a thump at the door splintered her reverie. She put down the piece of jewelry and wiped her hands on a cloth. Another thump and a scratching noise followed. When Carolina opened the door, the bell jingled and Fang trotted into the room leaving a trail of muddy footprints.

"Fang!" Thinking of several potent curses, she let the door go and turned to face the culprit. "You're all wet!"

"We're trying to get out of the rain." Will's voice surprised her. She pivoted toward the sound.

He seemed to fill the doorway. The sheer size of him always surprised her. Carolina's mind went blank for a few seconds. She felt as though she were seeing him for the first time all over again. Although this time, she knew what he smelled like, how it felt to have his arms around her, how warm and demanding his mouth could be . . . Carolina couldn't find a smile, or a nod, or a word of greeting. Will's face was in shadow, muting the color of his startling green eyes. His hair and the shoulders of his light jacket were wet, giving evidence to the fact that he was standing in the rain. "Fang, get back over here," he ordered. The dog obediently returned to the door. They both stood there looking expectantly at Carolina. "May we come in?" Will asked, but he didn't smile.

"Of course." Carolina found her voice, yet the words held the strained tone of politeness. *We have to start all over again,* Carolina reminded herself. *Pretend he's just one of the workmen. Someone who doesn't have any affect on you, or on your fantasies.*

But it was so good to see him. She returned to her chair at the workbench and watched as he wiped his boots on the mat, then slipped off his wet jacket and hung it on the doorknob. After instructing Fang to lie down on the mat near the door, he pulled a chair closer to the workbench and sat down.

He hadn't shaved that morning. The moisture on his face darkened the slight roughness of his beard, and Carolina's hand twitched with the urge to run her palm along his jaw to feel the texture.

"We can't work when it's raining like this," Will said, as if he was completely unaware of the effect his presence had on her.

"Oh?" Carolina managed. Her heart seemed to be pounding in slow motion, hard, heavy beats that made it difficult to speak without a quiver in the words. Searching for protection, and some way to postpone conversation for a moment, she slipped on her glasses, then picked up the piece of jewelry she'd been working on before he arrived. She'd thought she had her overreaction to Will under control. With him sitting across from her in the flesh, however, he was a good deal too close to ignore.

"We've gotten quite a bit of work done this week," he said as he casually picked up one of her mirror-finished hammers and turned it over in his hand. "The walls are framed in and the roof is partially finished." He returned the hammer to the table.

"Great," Carolina said noncommittally. In order to stay away from Will, she'd had to stay away from her new house, as well. She didn't want to have to explain why.

"So, how's your work going?"

Carolina looked at him then. He was trying to make conversation. She stared into his serious green eyes and suddenly wondered why, after days of avoidance, he was sitting in her studio . . . making conversation.

Will had missed her. As he watched Carolina's features change from composed to suspicious, he tried to appear innocent of any other thought besides friendly curiosity. But a few insubstantial hairs had come loose from her braid, and they curled along the pale skin of her neck like strands of dark silk. And what he really wanted to do was drag her into his arms and kiss her breathless.

After twelve days of staying busy and staying out of her way, he was about ready to climb the half-finished walls of her new house. And now the rain meant he couldn't work . . . and he couldn't stop thinking. And he'd come to the conclusion that he needed . . . Carolina. No matter if she fired him on the spot and ruined his reputation, he had to try one more time.

She picked up a pair of pliers. "I have one more main design to finish." She seemed to choose her words as carefully as her tools. "After that, whatever I get done will be surplus."

"May I see it?" He held out his hand.

Carolina placed the piece in his palm without touching his skin. The silver of the setting was still warm from her hands. He ran his finger over the pretty blue stone in the center of the abstract design.

"Careful, I haven't buffed down the edges of the bezel—the setting—yet. It might be sharp."

"It's really beautiful," he said, and meant it. He didn't know a damn thing about jewelry, but he knew quality, and Carolina's work was definitely quality. He handed the piece back to her.

"Thank you." She accepted it then gave him a questioning look, as if she expected him to leave or to state his intentions for being in her studio.

In a scramble for innocuous conversation, he looked down and noticed a bandage on one of her fingers. Without thinking, he reached for her hand and turned it palm up. "How'd you hurt your finger?"

"A close encounter with the polishing wheel," she admitted. Her voice sounded strained.

He ran his thumb over the slight callus below the bandage. "You need to be careful with these talented hands." Even as he said the words, his mind was on what other talents her hands might have. The thought caused his grip to tighten.

She tugged away her hand.

"Do you mind if I watch you work for a while?" Will asked. He wasn't ready to leave yet. Not until he found a way to make her smile again—to get past the silence that had grown between them for the past two weeks.

Surprise or wariness narrowed her brown eyes for a millisecond. But then she shrugged and went back to work. "Sure, I don't mind."

Will forced his gaze from her and looked around the room. He was having a problem letting go of Carolina. It had to be the challenge, the novelty of the situation that kept him tied up in knots when he couldn't see her, talk to her. Now, he would be content to watch her work. He wanted to know everything about her.

He picked up a tool that looked like a caliper but had a digital readout on the side. "What's this?"

"My favorite electronic miracle," she said with half a smile. "I can measure and read the digital numbers without my glasses."

He randomly chose one of her hammers, then glanced toward the mirrored surface of the anvil anchored to her left. "What's this?"

"It's a cross peen hammer—don't even think about it," she warned, seeming to read his intent. "None of my hammers hit the anvil without something soft in between." Will put the hammer back.

"What's this?" he asked, as he pulled the pliers she was working with out of her hand.

"Cut it out!" she said sternly, then she looked into his eyes and laughed.

Will felt like he'd been released from prison. Exonerated. A free man. A man with a bright future. A man in—

"Give me that," Carolina ordered, and held out her hand. Will played out the moment for as long as he could. She was still smiling, and he wanted her to hold that thought. He wanted to start at the beginning again. He wanted Carolina.

"What's for dinner tonight?" he asked, reluctantly handing over the tool.

Carolina's smile disappeared. She looked away as if she needed to count the implements on her workbench. "I haven't decided yet. Are you going to be here?" Her voice was calm, collected.

He would definitely be here. He couldn't stay away from her any longer. Sometime during one of his uncomfortable, sleepless nights in the toolroom, he'd decided he didn't give a damn what Brad thought, he was going to seduce Carolina. He wouldn't hurt her. He would help them both.

He'd started out wanting to help get her over her ex-husband, but now his own needs had gotten involved. He might not be a wealthy corporate businessman like her ex, or some movie-star actor. But he knew how to make a woman feel good, how to search out all the secret places that needed touching, that needed loving. He'd show Carolina what he could offer, how good it could be. Then, if that's all she wanted from him, he would handle it. He'd move on, just like he always had.

"I'll be here," he said, keeping his face perfectly blank.

"CAN I HELP?"

Carolina turned, startled by the close sound of Will's voice. This was the first time they had eaten together in two weeks, and Will seemed determined to make up for avoiding her by standing in her way every chance he got. It was almost comical.

"Here." Without missing a beat, she handed him a bowl of buttered potatoes. "You can put these on the table."

The sudden, pained look on his face surprised her.

"Ouch. It's hot," he said, gingerly placing the bowl on the counter.

"I'm sorry." Carolina fought back a smile. He had to be putting her on—the bowl hadn't burned her fingers. But just in case . . . She glanced around for the pot holder. Will was faster. He reached for the dish towel she had draped over her shoulder.

"I can use this." As he pulled the towel free, the back of his hand brushed against her collarbone, and a jolt of awareness sizzled through Carolina. Her urge to laugh evaporated.

He arched one questioning brow in her direction, as if he expected her to speak. When she didn't, he used the towel to pick up the bowl.

"Where did you say I should put this?"

Carolina did laugh then. She couldn't help herself. If he could have read her mind a moment before, he would have had a graphic image of where she'd like to put the potatoes. She gave his shoulder a flat-handed shove. "On the table. Unless you want to eat outside with Fang."

She was still smiling as she tossed the final ingredients she had chopped into a salad. Will was teasing her. Telling her to lighten up in his own way.

Why did she always have to take everything so seriously? Because she was older? Because she had learned the hard lessons of losing trust and foolish choices? Well, tonight was only one night in the history of the world, and she didn't want to think about lessons or choices. What was wrong with relaxing and laughing?

Nothing. And there was nothing wrong with enjoying Will's company instead of checking for motives in every word, every touch. He liked women. He liked her, she supposed. She could accept that.

And he had opened her eyes to the possibility that she might want a man in her life again at some point. Not a young gypsy who would be here and gone, but someone settled. Someone to laugh with over a hot dish of potatoes. Someone to hold her when she couldn't get to sleep at night. Even though she knew Will could never be *the* man in her life, he *was* sitting in her dining room.

Curiously lighter and more at ease than she'd been in a while, Carolina picked up the bowl of salad and a bottle of salad dressing and headed to the dining room . . . and Will.

For once in his life, Will was having trouble with his appetite. He was too nervous. He ate mechanically, but he'd lost interest in food as soon as Carolina had taken her place at the table across from him. She was smiling and relaxed, and he could barely remember what he'd eaten or how hungry he'd been.

Hungry . . . His normally healthy appetite had been overrun by another kind of hunger. And now that dinner was over, he could set his plan in motion.

"It's stopped raining," he commented casually as he helped pick up the dishes. "How about walking me home? I want to show you what we've done on the house." He held his breath.

"Okay," Carolina said. "Let me put these dishes in some water."

The twilight had nearly faded to black by the time they left the cabin. After the rain, the world outside seemed fresh and new, alive with the song of crickets. A mist of humidity hung in the air, and the beam from the flashlight in Will's hand made the trees appear shrouded, like ghosts stationed along the trail. Stars emerged through the ragged cloud remnants, promising a clear day when the sun returned. Right now, the darkness suited Will perfectly.

"It always smells so good after it rains," Carolina said, drawing in a long, slow breath. "No dust or pollen, just the clean smell of green."

"Yeah," Will agreed but his mind was on other words, other plans. "Listen, I want to apologize for the other day, and for how I've been acting."

His change of subject was met with cautious silence, so he continued, "I know you're all grown-up—" he slanted a half smile at her in an effort to keep the conversation friendly "—and divorced." He swung the flashlight to shine on the ground at Carolina's feet. It bounced back enough reflection for him to see her frown. *Here goes everything*, he thought. *Too late to turn back now.* "I know you must need a man around every once in a while. I just didn't think Kirkland was the right—"

"Oh, I don't know," Carolina interrupted. "If you look at it logically, Jimmy Kirkland is nearly the perfect man for me."

"What?" Will nearly dropped the flashlight. He stopped on the trail and faced her. "What's so perfect about him?"

Carolina continued walking, forcing Will to follow suit. "Well, let's see. He's at least five years older than I am." She hesitated for a moment. "He's been divorced long enough to want to find a woman who can cook and keep his house clean. He has a good business. He's settled in. Prescott is his home, so he wouldn't want to move."

Will had had all he could take. By the time Carolina got to, "His children are grown, and he likes to dance," he had grabbed her arm. "What about love...about making love? Does he turn you on?" He was fairly stunned by the idea.

Fang chose that moment to come racing down the trail. He brushed by Will's pant leg then pushed under Carolina's hand for some attention.

Carolina could have kissed the dog. His intrusion gave her the time she needed to resist Will's words, his touch. She was in danger of falling into the *serious* trap again. With a laugh prompted more by relief than joy, she pulled away from him and leaned down to scratch Fang's ear. "In the immortal words of Tina Turner, what's love got to do with it? Right, Fang?"

Fang didn't answer. Will didn't, either. Carolina straightened and compelled her feet forward along the trail as if nothing mattered but this evening stroll. Even though, for a few seconds, when she'd been caught by Will's demanding touch and his question about making love, she'd felt like she was standing on the ledge of a tall, tall building—in a stiff breeze. In eminent danger of flying, of falling, of saying what was really on her mind, in her heart. Afraid to admit the truth—that Jimmy Kirkland couldn't be much further from her idea of the perfect man unless he'd secretly been born on another planet.

It's better this way, she decided as she forced down the tide of longing that pulsed under her skin. Will wasn't her idea of the perfect man, either. But, when it came to the question of making love, Will would begin and end any wish list of candidates she composed. And she couldn't afford to wish. A shiver ran through her, and she rubbed her arms to ward it off. She could manage this.

She could see the house site looming in the dim beam from the flashlight. Will remained behind her, walking in silence as if she'd finally convinced him that Jimmy Kirkland was her ideal. Good. She wasn't sure how many more questions she could dodge. Plus, she reminded herself, Will had found his own perfect woman. Young and pretty and available—Carolina had seen her

with her own eyes. He would just have to be content
managing that woman's wants and needs.

"This is it," Will said, although his voice didn't con-
vey welcome. He seemed to have closed up into his own
thoughts. He walked through the door of the toolroom
and turned on the overhead light.

Carolina paused in the doorway. The space was
small, but Will had made good use of every centime-
ter. A rough workbench had been constructed along
one wall. Most of the heavy tools, like the drills and
chain saws, were neatly lined up underneath the bench
near the door. Toward the back of the room, a com-
fortable-looking pallet, which consisted of a foam mat
with a sleeping bag over it, had been arranged against
the wall. Carolina recognized the pillow by the color
of the pillowcase. It had been transferred from Will's
room in her cabin. A wooden crate stood next to the bed
with a book and a lamp on it. The room smelled of new
wood, sawdust and rain.

Carolina felt like a nosy landlady inspecting a ten-
ant's room. She didn't want to know whether he was
comfortable or not. She didn't want to see where he
slept and wonder if a woman had been cozily wrapped
up with him in his sleeping bag. Her mind seized on the
enticing fantasy of being naked, surrounded by his
warm arms, listening to the rain... She wanted to be
that woman.

"What do you think?"

"It's fine, I guess." She looked at him. "If you're more
comfortable here..."

Will held her gaze as her words drifted away. He had
no answer to the question of comfort. He'd sleep on a
bed of nails with the right enticement. And sleeping had
no part to play in his plans for the evening. Right now,

Carolina seemed hesitant about entering the room, about getting too close to him. He needed to solve that problem first.

"Come on—" he picked up the flashlight again "—let me show you the rest of the house."

As they walked through the darkness, Will resisted the impulse to take her arm. Instead, he shined the flashlight beam on the floor and stayed close. He took her to the vaulted living room area and aimed the light upward. Moving until his chest nearly touched her back, he pointed over her shoulder. "This is when the house is the most vulnerable. They managed to finish most of the roof decking on this side of the house before the rain." He shifted the light until it disappeared into the open sky. In the process he purposely leaned into her, bumping her shoulder.

She stepped away from him as if she'd been burned. "You still have a lot of sky left, though," he continued as if he hadn't noticed.

Carolina walked over to the demarcation line of the roof. One section of the floor was dry, the other wet.

"Will the rain ruin the wood?"

Will moved up behind her again, close. "No," he answered as the light gleamed across the wet surface. "One day of rain won't hurt it. The crew got part of the stairs framed in." He gave her arm a playful tug toward what looked like a hallway.

When they reached the framework, Will, in the guise of a gentleman, stepped aside to allow Carolina to go first.

Carolina realized her mistake when the light revealed that the frame for the stairs had been built, just as Will said, but the actual stairs didn't exist yet. That left her in a space the size of a closet with wood framing all around her and with Will standing in the only opening.

"Oh." She tried to laugh as she turned to face Will. "I thought we could go up the stairs." She started to move by him when his arm came up and blocked her path.

She stepped back.

Without touching her, he crowded her backward until she had nowhere to go. Then, with maddening slowness, he balanced the flashlight on one of the cross beams before he brought his hands up to rest on either side of her shoulders. He was close enough for her to feel the heat from his body. Close enough to kiss.

A sweet panic rose inside her, half fear, half pure heat. Didn't she know this would happen? Hadn't she felt this coming all evening? Now what was she going to do about it?

"Tell me what you want," Will demanded in a low voice, as if he could read the tumbling turmoil inside her.

With her spine pressed against the wood, she said the only part of the truth she could risk. "I want you to step back and give me a little room here."

A smile twisted across his mouth, but his eyes held hers with no mercy. "Why? Do I make you nervous?"

"Yes." Again, she was telling the truth, but it didn't seem to affect him.

His smile widened. He leaned closer, which barely seemed possible. "That's funny—you don't look nervous."

The first touch of his lips sent a schism of alarm through Carolina. Alarm quickly shifted to startled awareness, then to the fascinating discovery of the warmth and wetness of his mouth and how he was slowly tasting her, teasing her. Will was no inexperienced kid who needed to push or grasp or overwhelm to prove his point. He was a man who knew how to kiss, how to savor, how to make love to her mouth.

For the moment, Carolina gave in. The rush of pure, wish-fulfilling pleasure was stronger than her resistance, mightier than her logic. It leapt the tall fortress of her control and coaxed her to open to him, caused her to push one of her hands along his chest, made her wish she could stroke his bare skin.

At her touch, a tremor ran though Will and he deepened the kiss. Carolina felt a surge of delicious, reckless power, and her body quickened. She wanted to make him tremble. She wanted everything. His tongue teased and persuaded, and she welcomed each invasion with warm retaliation. Her mind filled with the vision of another kind of sensual invasion. Naked, body to body, skin to skin. The vision of where this kiss was leading the two of them. Of what she suddenly wanted more than anything. Will. She felt like she had leapt out of an airplane in order to discover if she could fly. Exhilarated . . . and out of control.

You know he'll leave you. The exhilaration faltered. *Are you strong enough to play the game, then watch him go?*

It took all her willpower to twist away from the sweet pleasure of Will's mouth. She ducked under his arm and squirmed past him.

"Don't leave, Caro." The broken sound of his voice stopped her in the doorway. She couldn't turn to face him. She felt him move up behind her and cringed. Goose bumps rose on her skin.

Will fought the craving to wrap his arms around Carolina, just to hold on, to give him a little more time to convince her. But if he did that, he might go too far. He knew he was balanced on an edge he'd never walked before. For one of the few times in his twenty-nine years, he wasn't sure what he might do if she ran away again. His mind was shell-shocked, his body humming. He wasn't even sure he could put two coherent words together at the moment. And he needed words, because if he touched her again . . .

"What's wrong with me?"

Carolina's shoulders shifted and straightened. He stared at the back of her head, trying to read her thoughts, willing her to turn around so he could look into her eyes.

"What?"

"I want to know what's wrong with me? Why you won't let me touch you?"

Finally, she turned to face him. She looked like a young girl, trying to act tough and grown-up. "Will—"

"I have to know what it is about me that you don't like—that scares you. Why won't you let me get close?"

"I'm thirty-six years old, Will. I'm flattered that you—"

"I don't give a damn how old you are."

Carolina took one small step away from him. "Well, I'm afraid I do give a damn. You're too young for me, and you're not the type of man I would get involved with. I've gone through a divorce, and if you're trying to make me feel better about it, I—"

"I'm trying to make us both feel better."

Her eyes widened as if he'd threatened to eat her alive. She turned and ran.

"Carolina!"

Will grabbed the flashlight and chased her. He caught her at the head of the trail. Fang, assuming he was part of the race, jumped around them barking. Will clamped his free hand firmly around Carolina's wrist and turned her to face him.

She was panting, out of breath, and he felt like his heart might explode. "I know what you need." His voice was harsher than he'd intended. He swallowed and tried to control the pounding of his heart. "I know how to make you feel right. Just let me . . ."

The stricken look on her face hit him like a blow. She didn't want him. She had confessed to needing a man, but she wasn't interested in him. The realization hurt more than he wanted to admit, even to himself. He'd tasted the passion in her, the heat. Who was it that could make her wild? The fence man? Her ex-husband?

Drawing in a long breath, he tried one more tack. He wasn't sure he could force the words out of his mouth, they hurt so much. He drew her hand up until he could kiss the center of her palm. Her hand was shaking. He pressed it against his jaw, looked directly into her honey-colored eyes, then shut the flashlight off and tossed it to the ground.

"In the dark, I can be anyone you want me to be."

8

A SHIVER RAN through Carolina, head to toe. *Will always finds a woman.* The warmth and slight roughness of his jaw underneath her palm caused her belly to draw and tighten. *Why not me?*

With steady pressure, he brought her closer, into his arms. He seemed to have run out of words, but he found her mouth unerringly in the dark. *He'll leave,* her mind reminded her as she opened to his tongue, as she gave herself to the hot prelude of his kiss. She waited for the rising fear to reply, to quench the feeling. To put a cold hand on her growing heat. *Not tonight,* her desire answered. She wouldn't let Will leave tonight. Tomorrow would have to take care of itself.

A murmur of surrender rose in her throat.

Will. Some part of her brain realized he'd been holding back, hesitating, when he'd kissed her before. Now he was serious, and the slow, sucking evidence of his undivided attention made her knees weak.

Will's warm breath teased her ear. Then he whispered, "Put your arms around my neck."

Light-years past the point of saying no, she did as he instructed. A moment later she was lifted from the ground, cradled in his arms. She pushed her face against his neck and breathed in the scent of him, soap and wood and heated skin. She'd wanted this for too many nights. She refused to think about where it would lead, about tomorrow or next week. Tonight, she didn't care where they were headed as long as she could hold on to Will.

Fang circled them in the darkness, giving out an occasional confused yelp, begging for attention. Carolina smiled into Will's shirt. *Sorry, Fang, he's mine tonight.* She shifted her fingers along the hard strength of Will's shoulder, then tightened her grip on his neck. *He's mine.*

WILL SHOULDERED the door to the toolroom shut in Fang's face. Then, leaning his back against the cool wood, he slowly lowered Carolina's feet to the ground. The light from the single overhead bulb made her eyes appear more gold than brown. Warm amber. He could have spent the next hour staring into those wide, mysterious depths, but she looked wary and unsure, even though her hands were on his arms, even though her mouth needed kissing. He reached around her and shut off the light.

He needed to kiss her again. If he kept kissing her, touching her, she would forget her wariness, he was sure of it. She would forget Jimmy Kirkland and her ex-husband. Hell, if he could get her to relax, she would forget what day it was.

Just don't stop, his mind ordered. *Don't give her time to remember any reason to run away again.* He separated his feet and pulled her between his spread thighs. His hand slid up the back of her blouse, warming her skin through the thin material. She settled against his chest and raised her hands to his neck, his face. Then she was kissing him. Will felt a new rush of hot blood gathering, tightening. *Come on, Caro*, he coaxed silently as he waited for her to experiment with just the right angle, the right pressure. When her tongue teased his mouth wider, asking, wanting, he complied.

With a bark and an impatient scratch at the door, Fang begged for entrance, as if he felt he should be included in any game Will and Carolina were playing. Carolina didn't appear to hear, and Will ignored him. But within a few minutes, the scratching became more determined and the barking more insistent.

Will dragged his mouth away from Carolina's long enough to bark his own command. "Beat it, Fang!" For good measure he kicked the door with the heel of his boot to punctuate the words. The scratching and whining stopped.

Carolina's mouth returned to his as if she needed his lips to breathe. He would have smiled if he hadn't been so damned turned on. He slipped one hand to the curve of her behind to pull her higher, because she seemed to be melting in his arms, languid and willing.

"Maybe we should lie down," he said, into her kiss.

"No, not yet. I want to touch you."

She met his mouth again, with more determination, and pulled at his shirt. Will lost his place in the sequential plan of gentle seduction. He rolled until her back was to the door, then helped her drag the tails of his shirt from his jeans.

When her cool hands stroked his warm belly, Will sucked in a sharp breath. He hadn't expected such an abandoned response. As her fingers explored his chest, Will fumbled with the buttons of his shirt. He managed to get the two bottom buttons undone before he realized he didn't give a damn about his shirt. He wanted to unbutton Carolina's.

She made a sweet, breathless sound when his hand found her breast. He tried to slow things down. He'd planned to whisper and kiss and caress, but before he realized it, he was pushing soft material off smooth, warm skin. And Carolina was helping him.

"Please, Will."

He heard her say his name, and a sharp ache of satisfaction ran through him. He wanted her to know who this was, even in the dark. He wanted her to remember how he could make her feel. Bending down, guided by his hand, he caught her nipple with his lips. He sucked, lightly at first, then harder. Her back arched away from the door. He pulled her hips tight against the aching swelling trapped by the barrier of his jeans. And discovered hers were in the way.

His hands went to work on the button at her waist as his mouth moved to her other breast. She was so sweet, so warm. He tugged each side of the placket in the denim and her zipper opened. Then his hand was inside, gliding across her smooth belly, into warmth and dampness.

He nudged her knees apart. "Let me . . ." His fingers slid lower, deeper. Carolina gasped and sagged against the door. "Hold on to me," he said.

Her hands gripped his shoulders and she pushed her face into his chest. He wished he could kiss her again, but he was too busy to rearrange their position. He was studying her reaction to the movement of his hand. He needed to find just the right spot.

A tremor ran through Carolina and she moaned. Her hips rotated, and her fingers dug into the muscles of his shoulders. In that moment he wanted to make her come more than he wanted to be inside her when it happened. They had all night for him to catch up.

Carolina suddenly came alive in his arms. No more resistance or shyness. One of her hands angled over his shoulder to his neck, then dragged his face down for a hot, openmouthed kiss. Just as Will congratulated himself on his control and his finesse, both her hands moved to the waistband of his jeans and began working the zipper open.

His erection seemed to grow tighter as the restriction of his jeans eased, and then Carolina's hands brushed him through the softness of his cotton briefs and he forgot about finesse.

He caught her hands.

"Wait, hon. We—"

"Please." Carolina pulled free and loosened the last buttons of his shirt. She wanted . . . No. Needed him now.

Right here, just like this. Maybe more than she'd ever wanted or needed anyone. The rush of urgency was scary, but Carolina was beyond stopping. She'd made her decision, faced her fear for this moment, this night. And she wanted all of it. Right now.

"No more waiting," she breathed, braver than she ever thought she could be. The skin of Will's chest, the chest she had admired for weeks, was smooth, and the slight roughness of hair teased her nipples as she pressed into him. She felt Will hesitate. His breath rushed along the side of her face. She didn't want him to say anything, not now. She wanted him to . . .

He shoved her jeans down her hips and thighs until she could kick them off along with her tennis shoes and underpants. Then he lifted her and drew her legs around his waist. The fire under his skin nearly burned her. She slid her arms around his neck and pressed closer into that heat. She wanted to be surrounded, to be filled.

"Hold on," he said. His voice was a harsh order in her ear as he fumbled with his own jeans. As soon as he was free, he fanned his hands flat against the door behind her and leaned her shoulders into them.

The first thrust took them both by surprise. There was no miscalculation, no awkwardness. They fit. Carolina sucked in a quick breath as sensation overtook her. No talking, no thinking, just feeling. She exhaled as Will withdrew and thrust again. So good. Just breathe and feel. Her body welcomed the shape of him, the size of him. The heat. A sheen of dampness appeared on Will's skin. His body was taut and he held her with silent, unerring concentration. Another slow thrust.

Carolina wanted to push, to arch with him, but she was suspended in the air between his hands and his hips. She squirmed and, out of frustration, ran her tongue along the damp skin of his neck to his ear. That got his attention. His mouth found hers, and as he kissed her deep and hard, he increased the movement of his hips.

Carolina, balanced on her own inner edge of climax, held on for dear life. As her body opened and the feeling escalated with the friction, her heart pounded with one rhythm. *Don't stop. Don't stop. Please don't—* She felt the first spasm of pleasure and moaned against his mouth. Her fingers dug into his skin, urging, pleading ... She broke away from his kiss to breathe, to center on the sweet, aching magic gathering around his thrusts inside her.

Will felt Carolina's body tighten and pulse, and his mind went fuzzy. He couldn't wait much longer. She was so tight and so lost in her pleasure. The pleasure he was giving her. He'd die before he'd come first. Will lifted one hand from the door and dragged her hips closer, faster, harder. Just as he passed the point of no return, she shuddered in his arms. She pushed her face tight into his shoulder. The low, recognizable sound torn from her made his belly clench, made the point of no return a distant memory. He braced her against the door, and with three emphatic thrusts reached his own breath-stopping climax.

Carolina felt boneless in his arms. He didn't want to pull out, to let her go yet, but the muscles in her thighs were trembling from their awkward position. Slowly, Will shifted her legs so that she could stand, but he held onto her in case she couldn't. Her face was still hidden, but he found her ear and kissed it.

"Are you all right?"

"Yes," she answered him, but she didn't look up. It was too dark to see her expression anyway. All he could do was listen to her voice. He angled one arm over her shoulders. "Balance me a second." He kicked off his boots and jeans somewhere in the vicinity of hers. Then he pulled her close to his hip. "Come on." She didn't say a word as he led her through the darkness to the pallet he'd been sleeping on for two weeks. He folded the top of the sleeping bag back, stretched out, then pulled her down next to him.

She still didn't speak as he covered her with the sleeping bag, and Will started to worry. Was she sorry? Did she think he'd taken advantage of her? He ran his fingers along her cheek and smoothed her hair, wondering what was going on inside her head.

Carolina wanted to crawl into a hole and hide somewhere. Embarrassed, she rested her cheek on the smooth skin of his biceps. Thank God Will had turned off the light. If she'd had to look into his eyes now, after proving how easily his touch could make her mindless, she'd cry. Maybe he'd done this a hundred times before, but she'd never lost control so intensely, so completely.

"Tell me what you're thinking."

Never, Carolina thought. But she had to tell him something. "I don't know what to say. What do you want me to—"

"You don't have to say anything." He leaned over her in the dark, until his lips brushed her cheek. "As a matter of fact—" he kissed the shell of her ear "—I'd rather touch than talk."

His lips brushed hers lightly. His mouth teased and nipped in a playful game that chased serious thought out of Carolina's mind. She smiled into the darkness. If he could be anyone in the dark, she could, too. She could pretend to be a twenty-year-old without a wrinkle, or a worry, or a past. She could put aside the fact that this touching, this loving would only last for one night. For right now.

"Stay with me tonight," he said between kisses.

Her fantasy of being naked, cozily wrapped in Will's arms, in Will's sleeping bag, had become reality. "Yes," she said without hesitating. She wanted to make the fantasy last as long as she could. To be surrounded, cradled in the pure maleness of him, the warm, physical comfort of skin to skin, breath to breath. Of his beating heart, close to hers.

Yes, her mind echoed as his demeanor changed from playful to persuasive, as his lips skimmed along her neck to her shoulder, to her breast. As he tugged on her nipple with gentle suction, her body rose to meet his mouth.

"Yes," she whispered to the darkness.

THE CHATTERING of birds woke Will. He slowly opened his eyes and drew in a breath. He could smell the faint fragrance of some feminine shampoo, sweet fruit— peaches or strawberries, maybe. He could smell the warm skin pressed against his chest and thigh. Carolina. They were lying together spoonlike, her back toward him. One bare shoulder and a cloud of dark hair were all he could see. He eased away and shifted onto an elbow in order to look at her.

One of her hands pillowed her cheek while the other rested just under the edge of the sleeping bag. She looked completely relaxed, as unafraid as a child. A wave of pure possessiveness rolled through him. This is where he wanted her, in his arms, his bed. Trusting and loving... He brought one hand up to pluck the band that had once secured her braid from the tangled strands of her hair. He pushed the hair away ʌom the tiny birthmark on her neck and did what he'd wanted to do for weeks. He pressed his mouth to the spot. Then his tongue.

Carolina mumbled something and raised her head slightly.

"Shh..." He kissed her ear. He knew they had to get up soon. The sky was growing lighter outside, and the men would be showing up to work. But not yet. It was light now, and he could see her. And she smelled too good, and he was too hard. And he wanted her willing in his arms one more time. He wanted to make damned sure she wouldn't forget the pleasure of spending the night with him. In case she woke up regretting. In case she ran away from him again.

Carolina struggled to consciousness. A pleasant, tired lethargy weighed down her limbs. She realized where she was and remembered what had occurred, but her mind floated, half aware of what to do next. What to say.

Will's warm hand moved along her waist, then drifted lower. The sleeping bag pulled as one of his knees nudged between hers. His fingers slipped into the warmth between her thighs, and her entire body seemed to awaken in a rush.

"Good morning," he whispered and lightly kissed her neck as if they were fully dressed. As if he wasn't stirring the very core of her into breathless chaos.

"Morning," she managed on a shaky breath. She tried not to move, to think of something to say or do, but she couldn't keep from shifting her hips under his hand. His fingers were sliding, ever so slowly, over the most sensitive part of her. He pulled her closer, and the hot length of his erection seemed to sear her skin.

She made an effort to turn in his arms, but he held her steady. "Be still. Relax."

Relax! Carolina would have laughed if the pleasure of his fingers hadn't robbed her of thought. As it was, she didn't want to do anything that would disrupt the moment, to stop the movement. She didn't want to think about the fact that she'd spent the night with him, the fact that the night was over and they were facing the revealing light of morning. She closed her eyes as he scooted her upward and slowly pushed inside her from behind. No need to think, not right now.

"ARE YOU SURE you're okay?"

Carolina ducked away from the fingers that were brushing her disheveled hair out of her face. She and Will were standing on the front porch of her cabin, and the morning sunlight was too bright. She couldn't look Will in the eyes. "I'm—fine," she answered, and chanced a quick glance upward. He was frowning. "I'm going to take a long hot shower, then I'll fix us some breakfast."

A truck rumbled down the road toward the cabin but made the turnoff to the new house. It was the second to arrive in the past few moments. Will glanced in the direction of the sound and sighed. "I'm not going to have time for anything but coffee. If I don't get back over there, someone will come looking for me."

Shortly after his thoroughly wicked wake-up call, Will had untangled himself from the sleeping bag, dragged on his jeans, then brought Carolina her clothes. After politely waiting outside for her to dress, he'd ushered her out of his room and to her cabin before any of the men reported to work. Carolina shuddered at the thought of being found naked with Will by the plumbers or the roofers.

"I'll put on some coffee now, before my shower."

Carolina turned to open the door but Will stopped her by putting his arms around her and pulling her against his chest. He seemed to know she didn't want to look at him, didn't want him to look at her this early in the morning with her sleepy eyes and wild hair. Sometime during the night, she'd lost the band that usually held her braid in order. A silly thing to think about now, but her mind was spinning in shocked circles. *What should I do? What should I say? What have I done?*

Will's arms tightened around her and he simply held on. His steady strength enticed Carolina to relax, and she leaned into him, although she didn't want to. She wanted to get some distance, some perspective. But it felt too good to just be held.

Finally, he loosened one arm and opened the door. "Go ahead, take your shower." His arms slipped away. "I can make the coffee. Oh, and here." Carolina glanced toward him. He pulled something from around his wrist and held it out to her. As he dropped her hair band into her palm, he smiled. "I like it loose," he said. "But I don't mind a little challenge."

His half smile faded as he stared at her in silent concentration. Carolina was suddenly afraid he might say exactly what he was thinking. That he was sorry. That they'd made a mistake. That it shouldn't happen again. "Thanks," she mumbled before she found her way through the door.

9

CAROLINA HAD TO HAND it to Mother Nature, she decided as she pulled the door to her studio closed behind her that afternoon. Hormones certainly had it all over celibacy.

It was a good thing she had the jewelry finished for the upcoming show in L.A., because although she'd managed to work most of the day, she'd found it difficult to keep her mind from wandering to certain moments of the night before.

Will hadn't been much help. When the crew quit for lunch, he'd made it a point to visit her. Without so much as an excuse me, he'd walked into her studio, taken the tool she'd been using from her hand, pulled her glasses off and kissed her until her entire body went into meltdown. Until she couldn't remember what she'd been doing before he walked through the door. And didn't care.

Goose bumps rose on her arms as she walked along the trail to the cabin, and it had nothing to do with the weather. The afternoon sun was warm enough. But Carolina's mind was on what would happen later, after dinner, when she and Will were alone together.

Her interminable logic interrupted. What if he had other plans? Maybe he had somewhere else to go. The memory of the kiss that had disrupted her entire afternoon overruled any attempt at being logical. Her instincts weren't that out of order. Will wanted to be with her tonight, he'd made that abundantly clear with his mouth and his hands, even if he hadn't said the words. And she wanted it, too. She hurried up the stairs of the cabin and went inside to start dinner.

"DO WE NEED to talk about this?" Will pulled Carolina closer and nuzzled her neck. He breathed in the scent of her hair and nipped the sensitive skin inside the collar of her blouse. She ducked toward him and her fingers dug into his shirt.

He traced a damp line of kisses to her ear while he waited for an answer. "No," she answered weakly. "I don't want to talk."

He smiled into her hair. He didn't want to talk, either. "I want to sleep in your bed tonight," he said as one of his hands casually worked the buttons of her blouse open. Carolina started to say something but seemed to lose the power of speech as his hand slipped inside the lacy cup of her bra. He lowered his head. "But it's not time for sleeping yet."

He got one quick glimpse of the soft pink shape of her nipple before his mouth closed over it. He wanted to see all of her, to take off her clothes piece by piece, touch by touch. With the lights on. He couldn't understand why, but he knew she wasn't ready for that yet.

As if she'd read his mind, one of her arms shifted and the lamp near the bed went out. He raised his head and looked into her eyes through the dimness. Was she still holding onto the illusion that he was someone else? Someone older, richer? Someone more like her ex-husband? For a few heartbeats he searched her face for the truth. But when her fingers gently touched his chin then eased along his jaw to draw him closer, he decided he didn't give a damn about the truth. Not right then.

WILL FELT the bed shift beside him as Carolina turned over. He knew it was early and, still pleasantly tired, he had absolutely no ambition to get out of bed. Carolina moved again and Will opened his eyes a fraction. She was naked, sitting on the edge of the mattress. The graceful, utterly feminine curve of her back and hips made part of him twitch and swell. The rest of him wanted to run his hands, his mouth over her smooth skin. But he didn't move. He watched as she stretched to pull her robe from the chair and was rewarded with just the briefest glimpse of belly and breast before she wrapped the material around her. He closed his eyes again as she turned so she wouldn't catch him ogling her like he'd never seen a woman before. When her footsteps receded, he yawned and glanced at the clock.

Work was the last thing he wanted to do today. Saturdays should be declared national holidays, as far as he was concerned. He wanted to spend the day with Carolina, doing something different, something fun. He wanted to get her away from the cabin and her studio, to see her relaxed and smiling. Before he made love to her again. His body reacted to the image, making his position painful. As he shifted his legs to get more comfortable, Carolina walked into the room.

"Morning," she said with a shy smile. She looked all scrubbed and bright-eyed. Will's erection pulsed once and grew harder. He tried to concentrate on innocuous subjects so his body would calm down. They'd made love more than once the night before, and he didn't want her to think he was intent on screwing her into the box springs. A little anticipation went a long way. Carolina sat on the bed next to him and bent over for a quick kiss.

Anticipation flamed. Instead of letting her sit up, Will pulled her into his arms. "I like your bed better than mine," he said into her hair. Memories of the night before hammered through his brain. Her shyness about letting him see her body. The sounds she made when she gave up control, when she let him stroke her over the brink. "Thank you for trusting me."

Carolina snuggled closer but didn't speak.

Will wasn't sure what he was supposed to say but he felt like he should say something. "I don't want you to think this happens with other clients." He frowned, unable to think of anything convincing. "You're different." Will was just beginning to realize how different — an unsettling thought. He'd never known anyone like Carolina. She was talented and smart and had a responsive body that made him want to groan. For a moment, his mind wandered to what it would be like to be loved by a woman like her. Loved, not screwed. He hadn't thought seriously about love for a long time.

Held suspended by that thought, Will lost the gist of the rest of what he intended to say. Almost of its own accord, one of his hands smoothed Carolina's hair, coming to rest on the braid at the back of her neck.

"I like your hair loose. Why do you always keep it braided?"

"Habit, I guess." Her voice sounded sleepy and content. "I work with power tools and annealing torches in the studio. It's too dangerous to leave my hair loose." She yawned. "You know? One of the first things I did after getting divorced was make an appointment to get my hair cut." Carolina remained relaxed against him. He was too comfortable holding her to worry about where the conversation might lead.

"Why?"

"I wanted to be different. I thought I needed to change, to leave behind the old, boring Carolina."

"And?"

A huff of laughter tickled the hair on his chest. "Luckily, at the time, my hairdresser was a man. He refused to cut it short. He said he'd regret it and I'd regret it, so I came out of there with a trim."

The thought of any man's hands in Carolina's hair made Will frown. He tugged on her braid. "I like it long."

"Me, too," she said. "But I had to figure that out on my own, regardless of someone else's opinion. It's funny how something as trivial as a haircut can make you realize that you've been living your life for the approval of others."

Will kept his hand moving over her hair, silently urging her to keep talking.

"That's why I'm building this house. I wasted years in a marriage where my husband's needs—his career and corporate image—always came first. Now, I'm choosing what I need for my home and my life. Permanence and stability."

"What about love? Do you still love him?" Will couldn't believe he'd asked the sixty-four-thousand dollar question. He tensed, waiting for her reaction. She shifted against him, and one of her hands skimmed across his chest.

"I did love him. . . . I thought everything was fine. I was so surprised when out of the blue he asked for a divorce." She turned her face, bringing her mouth closer to his ear. "Love is for idiots."

Will tightened his arms around her. "I'm sorry."

"Don't be." Her voice sounded sure again. She pushed out of his embrace, looked him in the eye and smiled. "I have my work. Soon I'll have a wonderful new house." Her lips met his for another quick kiss before she stood up. "Life is good."

Life is amazing, Will thought as he gazed into her smiling face. He wanted her again, right now. It was all he could do not to tug her into bed next to him. It would take him about thirty seconds to get her interested.

And he was already halfway there.

"Let's take the day off," he said. "Go do something fun." If he stayed in her bed much longer, they'd never even make it downstairs. He searched for some neutral idea. He hadn't had much free time to explore the city of Prescott, but one of the plumbers had mentioned horses—that Prescott was famous for its rodeos and horse racing. "How about going to the horse races?"

"I'd love to, but I really shouldn't."

Will sat up and swung his legs to the floor. He kept the sheet strategically resting over his groin. Carolina stuttered to a halt. Will grinned at her.

After rolling her eyes at his naked impertinence, she turned her back to him and busied herself with something on her dresser. "I have to get everything labeled and packed for the show. I'm leaving day after tomorrow."

Leaving day after tomorrow. The idea finally penetrated. Carolina wouldn't be here after tomorrow night. She'd be in L.A. For once a woman was actually leaving him behind, and he didn't like it much. The truth startled him. He reached for his jeans, then stood up to pull them on.

"I'll help you get packed."

Carolina faced him again. He dredged up a smile, wrapped his arms around her in a playful bear hug, then lifted her until her feet were dangling. "Let's go enjoy ourselves." He bit her neck lightly while she squirmed.

"Okay, okay," she said, giving in with a half groan, half laugh. "Let me go, and get out of here so I can get dressed."

"Works every time," Will said as he lowered her feet to the floor. "Sweep a woman off her feet and she'll follow you anywhere."

In the next few seconds, Carolina went completely serious on him. It was on the tip of his tongue to ask what he'd said wrong, but she spoke first.

"Go down and make coffee," she ordered with a smile that didn't quite look happy. "Before I change my mind."

Sweep a woman off her feet. Carolina watched Will disappear through the doorway of her bedroom, then slowly sank down on her dressing stool. She'd been swept, all right. She'd opened the lid on a Pandora's box of sexy treasure, and now she was in trouble. She hadn't expected to enjoy the sensation quite so much.

He was a good lover. But more than that, he was loving. Paul had never been loving. He'd been demanding and in control, sexy in a macho sort of way... but never giving and considerate. Will seemed to be excited about sharing pleasure, about every body part having a good time. His unabashed enthusiasm made her smile. And it made her crazy.

Don't get too attached. You know he's going to leave. And you're not following him anywhere. Carolina shrugged away her voice of doom. She was glad she'd taken a chance with Will. No matter what happened later, she wanted to enjoy him while it lasted.

10

"DEAD LAST." Will couldn't seem to contain his merriment. Carolina smacked his arm with the racing form. It wasn't her fault. She'd never claimed to be an expert on quarter horses, and Li'l Roper looked as likely to win as any of the other entries.

She and Will were leaning against the railing at the back of the low-slung wooden grandstand that overlooked the finish line. This racing facility, compared to the one Carolina had visited once in southern California, was like the difference between AAA baseball and the major leagues. No escalators or air-conditioning. No padded seats. Just serious horse-racing fans and a rough track. She loved it.

Will leaned closer than he needed to and asked, "Who've you got picked for the next race?"

A leading question if she'd ever heard one. She angled back to look into his eyes. "Why?"

His mouth twitched into a smile. "Well, there's no sense losing all our money at once. We should at least make it last a few more races." His green eyes sparkled, and Carolina raised the program to hit him again. Instead of ducking, though, he bent close, his mouth stopping a few inches from hers. Carolina forgot about hitting him and automatically raised her chin to be kissed, a new and very rewarding response she'd learned in the last day or so. Will laughed. His warm breath tantalized her lips, but he didn't kiss her.

"What?" He teased, waiting, as if he required her to ask, to acknowledge what she wanted. She wanted to be kissed. She completed the connection by grabbing his collar to pull him forward. She pressed her mouth to his, oblivious to the people walking by and the scattered spectators in the seats around them. As if to prove he was more than willing to participate, one of Will's hands slid upward, along her arm from elbow to shoulder. A shiver followed in the wake of the contact.

"Carolina!" A woman's voice penetrated the private haze surrounding the two of them. Will pulled back from the kiss. Suddenly, Carolina was facing her friend Sue Ann and her husband, James, along with two other people she'd never met. Caught off guard for a moment, Carolina didn't know how to respond.

"What are you doing here?" Sue Ann asked. Her gaze riveted to Will, running head to toe.

Carolina glanced from Sue Ann's speculative gaze to her husband's disapproving frown. The scalding surge of a blush flamed up her neck. They'd seen her kissing Will. She felt like a teenager who'd been caught in the back seat of a car. "I— We're—" She hadn't been prepared for this. She and Will had been so lost in their own little world. . . . Carolina took a deep breath and tried to form a reasonably normal-looking smile. One of her hands rose to touch Will's arm, to include him, and also to steady her equilibrium. "This is Will Case." She turned to him, feeling miserable. "Will, this is my friend Sue Ann and her husband, James. And—" She glanced toward the other couple.

Sue Ann completed the sentence. "This is Linda and Ray, friends of ours from Phoenix. We're showing them the high points of living in the wilderness." She laughed.

Will politely nodded to the women, shook hands with the men. He didn't seem ill at ease, yet Carolina could feel his eyes on her, as if he was waiting to follow her lead.

"I'm surprised to see you two here today," Sue Ann said sweetly, and Carolina could have kicked her. "Aren't you leaving for L.A. soon?"

"Day after tomorrow," Carolina answered. "I have everything finished and packed. We were just—" Her mind showed her an instant replay of what she and Will had *just* been doing—kissing. "We decided to take a little break."

Sue Ann gave Will a look that said there was nothing little about it. Curiosity in full flight, she said, "We're on our way over to the Lariat steak place. Why don't you guys come along?"

"No." Carolina couldn't get the word out fast enough. "Thanks." She glanced at Will, searching for moral support. "We have to . . ."

"Get back before the roofing crew leaves for the day," Will supplied smoothly.

"Right." Carolina shrugged, as if the entire matter was out of her control. "Maybe next time."

"Well, you two have fun," Sue Ann added as a parting shot. With a wave and a Cheshire-cat smile, she took her husband's arm and led him toward the exit.

Carolina watched them walk away feeling like all the fun had been sucked out of the afternoon.

"Is there a problem?"

"No," Carolina answered quickly. Will was frowning, and she felt as if she'd betrayed him somehow. Like a lecherous older woman showing off her willing, younger stud. She'd never intended to put him on display, yet that's how it had ended up. "No problem." She kept her voice light. She forced her eyes to the program in her hand. "Who should we bet on in the next race?"

Will watched Carolina's struggle to act nonchalant and fought the urge to swear. She'd been laughing before, and kissing him. Now she looked like she wanted to cry. Was introducing him to her friends so embarrassing? He knew her ex-husband was some kind of corporate executive. Was she ashamed to be seen in public with a mere contractor? A man who worked with his hands?

His ego spoke before his better judgment could stop it. "Maybe we should skip the next race. Are you about ready to go?"

She looked at him then. "I'm sorry. I guess we should. We've managed to waste most of the day. I suppose we'd better get back." She tried to smile.

Damn. Way to go, Will. He'd offered her an escape and she'd hit the door running. He confiscated the program from her hand, tossed it into the garbage, then took her arm. *Way to go.*

CAROLINA SIGHED as she looked out over the valley. The rocks beneath her were still warm from the sun, although the air was cooling off. Behind her, in the distance, she could hear occasional voices and the noises of construction. She and Will had arrived home before the crews packed up, although the real reason for coming back weighed on her mind.

It was time to slow down the roller coaster and take stock of the situation. What was she doing with Will? What exactly did she want from him? Sex? Was that it? Suddenly, every one of her thirty-six years seemed to be balanced squarely on her shoulders. How had she thought she could blithely introduce Will as her lover when she couldn't even undress in front of him with the lights on?

She'd gone into this affair with the rationalization that Will was used to short-term, no-hard-feelings relationships. That if he wasn't in her bed, he would've been in some other woman's. And that rationalization had been fine in the heat of the moment.

But today, when she'd been forced to introduce him to her friends, when she'd seen their reaction, she'd felt unscrupulous. If she didn't know Will, if he was merely a stranger, a one-night stand, she might have been able to take the whole thing lightly. But this was Will, her brother's best friend. The man who had kidded her, who had helped make her dream house a reality. The man who had made her realize she still had a measure of passion inside. She couldn't pay him back by allowing her friends to snicker behind sly looks and unkind gossip. They could say what they wanted about her—she deserved it, but Will didn't.

"Hey, boss lady."

Carolina jumped at the sound of his voice. She had to shade her eyes from the lowering sun to see his face. "Hey."

He climbed up the rocks to find a spot near her. "What are you doing out here all alone?"

"Thinking," she answered.

"That sounds like a bad sign." He braced his arms on his knees and waited as patiently as a therapist.

"I want to apologize for what happened at the races today."

"Which part?"

Carolina gave him a level look. "The part about my friends looking at you like you're a walking hunk of meat at my disposal."

He shrugged and gazed out over the valley. "I know what most women want from me, and it has nothing to do with my heart. And I've been the available male before. Granted, it's been awhile." His mouth twisted with a slight smile. "I've learned to be a little more choosy in my old age."

"But I don't want you to feel—"

He claimed her attention with an exasperated stare. "Carolina, I don't give a rat's ass what your friends think. I only care about what you think."

Will watched as Carolina's spunk seemed to wilt right before his eyes. She dropped her gaze to her clasped hands and sighed.

"Were you embarrassed for your friends to see us together?"

"Yes. A little."

The look on her face said, *more than a little*. A band of apprehension tightened across Will's chest. *Here it comes*, he thought. "Why?"

The sadness in her brown eyes made him want to hit something. "I thought I could do this, that we could... I thought after one night, when the challenge was over, you would lose interest. You'd find someone else."

"Why would I do that? And why would that embarrass you?"

"Because there are so many other women your age and I'm—"

"Older. So?"

"So, I don't have the body—or the face—of a twenty-year-old. I know it. My friends know it. And you know it."

"Is that what you think it's all about with every man? Numbers and measurements?" He didn't want to argue with her, but he sure as hell wasn't going to sit there and let her tell him what he thought. "What about the way a woman moves, or the sound of her laugh? What about the way she looks you in the eyes when she's talking? And her voice when she whispers in your ear?" He couldn't hold back a sound of disgust. "Your ex-husband didn't corner the market on being an ass. But if you think the rest of us are checking birth certificates and asking dress sizes, you're wrong."

"But age is different."

"No." Will rubbed a palm down his face and searched for the right words. "Listen. I've had my hands or my mouth on almost every part of your body." He made an attempt at a smile. "The important parts, anyway. And if you think at this late date that I'm suddenly going to discover something old about you, you're nuts. And if your friends think I'm too young for you, tell them to mind their own business." He crossed his arms over his chest and challenged her. "That's what you're always telling me . . . That is, unless you have a problem with it."

Carolina stared at him for so long he thought she might be contemplating murder. "What am I supposed to think about what we're doing? What people are saying? You're the same age as my brother, and we both know what's going on between us is temporary."

"It feels pretty good right now, doesn't it?" Will captured one of her hands, brought it to his mouth and kissed her palm. The concerned look on her face made his chest hurt. He didn't know what to tell her. He only knew he wasn't ready to consider ending what they had started. Not yet.

"You think too much as it is. Let's take it a day at a time. A night at a time." He softened the words by pulling her forward until she was sitting between his

knees. He held her against his chest, close enough to
kiss. Then he playfully cuddled her until she relaxed.
"Let's go back to the cabin. I could cook you dinner for
a change."

Carolina began to laugh. Will pretended to be out-
raged by her opinion of his talent in the kitchen. "Hey,
it isn't that funny!"

"HAVE YOU GOT any candles?" Will grabbed the dish
towel Carolina was holding and waited for an answer.

"Yes." She stopped to remember where they might
be. "There are three or four on the mantel." She squatted, opened the bottom drawer of the kitchen cabinet
and dug out two more. "What are you going to do?" she
asked as she handed them to Will.

His lips formed an innocent smile that wouldn't fool
a nun for a second. "Science project," he said.

"Wait a minute . . ."

Will awarded her a chaste kiss and a little push toward the door. "I want you to take a nice hot shower.
Shave your legs—" he waggled his eyebrows in a poor
imitation of Groucho Marx "—or whatever you do.
Then put on something pretty. I'll be waiting for you
upstairs." His smile disappeared.

As Carolina stood there, caught by the promise, the
hunger in Will's eyes, her insides seemed to rise and flow
into a slow, warming somersault. Her body heated,
toes upward, and she had the ridiculous notion that she
would rather stay there and just stare at his face. She
couldn't remember anyone ever looking at her in quite
that manner, and she wanted to savor the moment, save
the memory. She knew he would leave. But not tonight
or tomorrow. And no matter what happened, she

wanted to remember every sweet second, every touch, every kiss. Every heated look.

Will had other things on his mind, it seemed. He lowered his chin and nodded toward the door. "Go on. I'll finish here."

It took her longer than it should have to find the sexiest gown she owned—a teal blue scrap of silk with spaghetti straps that crisscrossed the open back. She'd bought it on a whim and then never worn it. It was still wrapped in tissue paper in the bottom of her underwear drawer.

As she took her shower, she refused to think of tomorrow or next week. One night at a time, he'd said.

It was dark downstairs when she came out of the bathroom. The upstairs hallway shimmered in the glow of flickering light from her bedroom.

Carolina stopped in the doorway and gazed into her own bedroom as if she'd never seen it before. Because of Will . . . Everything was different because of Will. He'd placed lit candles on the dresser and her nightstand, and he was reclining on the bed, his back propped by pillows piled against the headboard, wearing nothing but a smile and an abbreviated pair of boxer shorts. Without taking his gaze from hers, he swung his legs over the edge of the bed and stood up. And opened his arms.

He kissed her once, slowly and too briefly from Carolina's point of view. He cradled her face in his big hands and looked at her.

"Do you trust me?"

She trusted him with her house, her body. But she didn't trust him not to leave. She gave him a one-night-at-a-time answer. "Yes."

He kissed her again, a little longer this time. But, when she responded, he dragged his mouth away. He walked to the bedroom door and closed it. The reflection of his strong shoulders and muscular chest in the full-length mirror on the back of the door made the rhythm of Carolina's breathing change. He pulled the short stool situated in front of her dressing table over until it, too, was reflected in the mirror. Then he sat down.

"Come here."

It didn't sound like an order. It sounded like a plea. Carolina would have done anything he asked if he asked her in just that way every time. A small niggle of alarm went off inside her. He wouldn't ask her to love him. He couldn't make her. *One night at a time.*

He pulled her between his spread knees and turned her until she was facing her reflection in the mirror.

"I want you to see how beautiful you are," he said, his voice shaky, as if he'd taken in too much air. "I want both of us to see."

Then his fingers were in her hair, loosening the braid, arranging the soft, cool strands over the warm skin of her shoulders and neck.

When he was satisfied with her hair, Carolina watched his strong hands run over the blue-green silk until they spanned her waist. "You feel so . . . smooth." His fingers moved in circles, tantalizing, shimmering across the cool material, caressing the skin beneath it. Carolina sucked in a long breath, entranced by the sight of those hands and the rough timbre of his voice.

He leaned into her, bringing his solid chest against her behind. His hands slid upward, stretching the silk at the swell of her breasts. Carolina observed as her nipples rose and pushed against the fabric—aching for his touch. Greedy. Her eyes drifted closed, she wanted to feel, not watch.

"Open your eyes, Caro."

His fingers were gliding up her arms now, to her shoulders. He hooked a thumb under one of the insubstantial straps of her gown and slowly pulled it over her shoulder, pushing her hair out of the way. He coaxed her to raise her arm, but as the gown sagged, exposing her right breast, she tensed.

"Will—"

"Shh." He covered her pale, bare breast with his sun-darkened hand and kissed the exposed skin of her back. "I want us to see together."

"Will, I—"

"Look at me."

When she met his gaze in the mirror, she saw determination . . . and desire. He wasn't undressing her for sport. He was dead serious.

"Trust me." His voice was little more than a whisper.

She wanted to. She had to, because the other strap was sliding downward. Carolina kept her gaze on his hands as they caressed, explored. She could feel his warm breath to the left of her spine. When he had satisfied himself with the exploration of her breasts, he pushed the gown lower on her hips.

The sight of his large hand splayed across her belly made Carolina gasp. His hands never stopped moving, and soon the gown was a pool of color at her ankles. There was no time for embarrassment. She couldn't worry about a few extra pounds or thirty-six-year-old thighs. He was telling her with his eyes and his hands that he wanted her, all of her.

His fingers eased between her thighs, and Carolina thought she might fall down. He put one arm high, around her waist, to keep her upright. In the middle of the excruciating fear and pleasure, Carolina chanced one look at the reflection of her face, softly etched by the candlelight and the pleasure Will was giving her. For that one millisecond, she did feel beautiful.

A moan was torn from her as Will's fingers became more determined. Her eyes closed. Will turned her in his arms, as if he'd decided she'd had enough of the game, and pressed his mouth to her breasts, kissing each, then sucking while holding her tight against his chest.

Carolina had to dig her fingers into his shoulders to hold on. His mouth was so hot and wet on her skin, and she wanted to get closer, to press harder.

Will shoved the stool backward and sank to his knees in front of her. And, just as Carolina decided that she'd had all she could take, he pressed his open mouth to the center of her sex.

Will was beyond thought. The look on her face as she watched his hands making her hotter and hotter nearly pushed him over the edge. He'd never been rough before. He knew how to do things without hurrying. But right now his body was so primed, and she was so ready. He pushed his mouth snugly into the springy curls between her legs and tasted her with his tongue. He wanted to lick and suck until she screamed, then maybe she'd know how much he wanted her—every part, every inch.

She was making low sounds now, sounds that made his skin feel scalded. A little bit more, a little harder. Her body bucked in his arms, and she bent over him, scraping his back with her nails. A shudder ran through her, and he could feel her convulsions from his tongue to the soles of his feet.

Carolina seemed to be melting in his arms. He had to shift his position to keep her from sliding to the floor. He pushed to his feet, picked her up and placed her on the bed. She pulled him down, burying her face against his neck. He kissed her ear, her neck, her cheek. He tried to ease her back so he could look into her eyes, but she seemed to be intent on hiding.

He ran his hands down her body. He wasn't sure how much longer he could wait. He slid one hand over her mound.

"Caro, open for me, let me—"

Her hands tickled down his chest. He drew in a sharp breath, and the muscles of his stomach jerked as they slid lower. She was pushing off his boxers, pulling him over and down. Inside. She sighed into his ear and nipped the lobe with her teeth. "So good..."

He nearly lost it before, with one strong thrust, he got inside her. The rest became a blur of tight and hot and rough. When he came, it was backbreaking, toe-curling, and a hell of a lot better than it was supposed to be.

11

FANG'S DETERMINED BARKING woke Carolina. She rolled over and bumped into Will as he sat up. "Sorry." She pushed her hair out of her face. Groggy and disoriented after the intense physical and emotional nature of the night before, she couldn't even remember what day it was.

"Sounds like someone's here," Will said as he pulled on his jeans. He didn't bother with a shirt.

"What time is it?" Carolina managed.

"Nine-fifteen."

"Nine-fifteen!" Carolina moved to edge of the bed and reached for her robe as Will gave her a quick kiss and left the room. She couldn't believe they'd slept so late. No wonder one of the crew had come over to find Will. She shook her head to clear it. What she really needed was a long, wake-up shower.

As Carolina walked down the stairs, she could hear voices. The fact that she didn't have anything on under her robe slowed her down for a moment, but she knew Will wouldn't invite any of the workmen into the cabin. She'd feel a lot better if she could sneak into the bathroom without being noticed.

Carolina stopped midway down the stairs when she realized Will *had* invited someone inside. Before she could gracefully retreat, she was staring into her brother's surprised face.

Brad remained speechless long enough for Carolina's entire body to blush. Her hands automatically went to the edges of her robe to pull it tighter around her.

"What's going on here?" Brad asked, his voice tight with incredulous suspicion.

Carolina's eyes skipped to Will for a second before she answered. She knew her brother's opinion of Will's success with women. And she also knew Brad wouldn't be happy to know Will had been successful with her. "What do you mean?" She searched for the peevish voice of a big sister to brazen it out. "I'm sorry. I forgot you were coming in today and overslept. So, sue me."

Brad gave Will a hard look. Will just shrugged, but Carolina could see the tightness in his body. She couldn't stand the thought of Brad and Will arguing or even discussing *her*.

"What's the problem?" Will asked his best friend.

"I thought you were sleeping in the new house," Brad said.

"Since when are you so concerned about where I sleep?"

"Oh, please," Carolina huffed as she came down the stairs. "Will slept in his room upstairs last night. What's the big deal?" She couldn't look at Will to see how he was reacting to her lie. She had to hope he'd corroborate what she said to prevent a scene. "I'm going to take a shower. Why don't you two make some coffee?" Without another glance she walked into the bathroom and shut the door.

It was some of the best acting she'd ever done. She'd managed to lie to her brother and coerce Will into going along with the lie in one desperate motion. So why did she feel like crying? She'd always been dependable, responsible Carolina to the men in her life. If Brad found out about her and Will, he'd probably think she'd completely lost her mind.

By the time she'd taken a shower and gone upstairs to dress, Will and Brad seemed to have moved on to other topics over coffee. Both men looked up when Carolina entered the dining room after filling her own cup and putting some muffins in the oven to heat. Brad, in a mood more like his usual self, stood and gave her a perfunctory buss on the cheek.

When Carolina looked at Will, she felt like she'd boarded an elevator that was plunging downward. He'd gone upstairs and finished dressing at some point. Now he was watching her with somber eyes full of questions like, "What the hell am I supposed to do here?"

"Sorry about this morning," Brad said as he sat down. "I was just surprised to see you…" He shrugged and grinned toward Will. "I should have known better but I—"

"How long did it take you to get here from Phoenix?" Carolina asked, changing the subject as swiftly as she could.

Brad launched into a description of his flight out and the hour-and-a-half drive from Phoenix. Carolina asked polite questions occasionally, but Will remained silent. When they'd eaten muffins and the conversation had stalled, Carolina looked at Will.

"Why don't you take Brad over and show him the new house?"

Will held her gaze a little longer than necessary before slowly pushing to his feet. "Sure." He didn't look particularly happy about it.

Carolina forced a smile toward her brother. "I'll walk over in a bit." She felt like she might self-destruct if she didn't get away for a few minutes to collect herself. *How are you going to deal with this?* her mind wailed. She could see by the look on his face that Will was angry, or at the very least, confused. Why had she forgotten about her brother coming to visit?

As the front door closed and quiet flowed around her, Carolina knew why she'd forgotten about Brad. She knew why she'd forgotten about her upcoming show, her new house, about everything. Because of Will. She balanced her elbows on the dining room table and covered her face. What was happening to her? Was she so lonely that the first man who came along and pressed the issue could take over her life? She'd almost had a heart attack when Brad had jumped to the right conclusion earlier. What did that mean? She couldn't have it both ways. She couldn't have Will in the dark then deny what they were doing during the day. But what was the point of getting everyone upset? Will was temporary—they both knew that going into this. So why should they present themselves as a couple when they were only lovers?

Only lovers . . . Carolina's mind shifted to the night before, to the loving way Will had looked at her, touched her. It hadn't been just sex. They had made love. Love . . .

Tears overflowed and dripped into the palms of her hands. An ember of anger flared. *I don't love him. I won't love him!* She swore vehemently. *I can't make him stay, and he can't make me love him.*

SOMEHOW THEY MADE IT through the day and through dinner. As the evening progressed, however, the conversation seemed to grow more stilted. In the middle of one of the lulls, Carolina decided to make some coffee just to have something to do. To get out of sight, out of the aim of all the simmering questions balanced between her and Will. She was in the kitchen when the phone rang. Brad answered it.

Judging by the look on Brad's face as he handed her the receiver, Carolina figured someone had died.

"It's Paul," he said.

Carolina's gaze immediately shifted to Will. The look on his face nearly stopped her heart. Unable to do anything else, she put the phone to her ear.

"Hello, Paul."

"How have you been?" he asked in a neutral voice, like he was merely an acquaintance who'd called to say hello.

"I'm fine," she answered in the same neutral tone.

But she wanted to shout at him. *Why did you have to call now? I don't want to talk to you!* She couldn't look at Will again, and she knew Brad would be frowning. She kept her eyes on the bloodred diamond woven into the center of the Navaho blanket draped over the chair.

"I saw the notice for your show in L.A. this week." He paused. "I thought we might get together for dinner one night while you're here. Where are you staying?"

Just like that, he thought they would get together. She'd always been accommodating. Why would he think she'd changed? Because they were divorced? Because he'd traded her away like a car with an expired warranty?

"I don't know, Paul."

Will got to his feet and said something to Brad. Carolina turned, switching her concentration to their conversation.

"I didn't sleep well last night," Will said. His attention settled on her for a moment. Gone was the smiling, playful lover. The distance between them might have been five light-years instead of five feet. "And I have to get up early." His gaze probed hers, then he turned.

"Will?" she managed.

He stopped and looked at her. But Carolina's mind seemed empty of words. She had no idea what to say. And Paul was speaking to her again, asking her something.

"Good night," Will said.

Carolina watched in silence as Will shut the front door a little harder than necessary and went to his room in the new house.

"I THINK Will is pissed that I thought he was messing with you," Brad said a few minutes later, after she had gotten off the phone.

Carolina realized she was staring at the door Will had just walked through. Of all the things that needed to be talked about, this was one discussion she was determined not to have. "You know, one of these days you're going to have to learn to mind your own business."

"What did Paul want?"

"Brad!"

"Humor me," Brad said without a smile. "If Paul's trying to jerk you around again, I may make a little visit to L.A. myself."

"Beyond asking me out to dinner, I don't know what Paul wants. And I don't care." As she said the words,

Carolina felt a rush of relief. She really didn't care. But she could see by the stubborn expression on Brad's face that he didn't believe it.

Irritated with her little brother, she stood up. She was more worried about what Will believed than about Brad or Paul. "I think I'm going to bed, too. I need to get up early and double-check that I haven't forgotten anything before I leave tomorrow." She stopped at the foot of the stairs. "You know where everything is. I'll see you in the morning."

After pacing around her room a few times, Carolina ended up at the window, staring into the darkness. She needed to talk to Will. How could she leave the next day without saying goodbye? Without saying...something.

A moment later she heard Brad's footsteps in the hall. She waited another forty-five minutes to give him time to settle in and go to sleep before she sneaked down the stairs and out the front door.

The house site seemed unnaturally still in the darkness. Carolina played the light from the flashlight over the trail in front of her and suffered an uneasy thought. What if Will had gone?

Before she could come up with an answer, a large hand came down on her shoulder. With her heart in her throat, Carolina spun around, not knowing if she should fight or flee. In the process, she dropped the flashlight.

"Will!" Her heart was pounding so hard she could barely speak. She slipped her arms around his waist and pushed her face into his shirt. "You scared me."

Will just stood there without returning her embrace. His posture seemed alert but not welcoming. Carolina loosened her arms. The flashlight on the ground gave enough reflection for her to see that Will didn't look happy to see her. He looked furious. She slowly dropped her hands away from him and stepped back.

"You looking for me?" he asked in a tight voice. "It's dark now. Nobody can see us. Is that why you're out here?"

Carolina swallowed and had to fight the anger that seemed to radiate from him like heat from a stove. The prickling warning of tears made the backs of her eyes hurt, but she wasn't going to let him believe that she was ashamed of him.

"I'm sorry." Her voice quavered and she had to swallow before continuing. "I didn't know what to say to Brad. He's so—"

"Sorry doesn't cut it," Will snapped. Suddenly his hands had captured her shoulders and he was staring into her upturned face. "If you're too embarrassed to admit that I've touched you—" he shook her once "—that I've been inside you, then stay away from me." A bleak look narrowed his eyes. "Don't come looking for me when no one's around."

"Will—" Carolina's voice broke. She couldn't control the tears that flooded her eyes. When he started to move away, she threw her arms around him. "Please listen to me." He hesitated, and Carolina tightened her grip.

"I don't know how to do this," she sniffed. "Tell me how it works. Tell me how to explain to my brother that we're . . . lovers." Will's chest expanded as he drew in a long breath. Carolina thought that if he didn't put his arms around her soon she would die.

"I can't leave with things like this between us," she continued in a blind search for an answer.

His hands came up to grip her head and tip it back. Carolina looked into his hard features and let her whole body relax into his grip. "Tell me," she whispered, unable to fight or to argue anymore.

Will's mouth descended on hers like a starving man on his last meal. He didn't tell her anything. He had no rights when it came to Carolina. She hadn't even admitted to Brad that they were involved.

And he was gutted by the thought of her seeing her ex-husband again.

He needed to show her. He needed to get inside her clothes and make her realize that the attraction between them was strong. Too strong to keep it a secret for very long.

Carolina made a sound. Of surrender, of longing or just of lust, he couldn't tell. But he knew she was leaving tomorrow, and he intended to give her something other than her ex-husband to think about while she was gone.

WILL CROWDED Carolina down onto his sleeping bag and began removing her clothes. He wanted to feel her skin, all of it, head to toe, pressed against him. She raised her hips so that he could shove her jeans down and off, then her hands were on the buttons of his shirt. He wanted to point out that even if she was embarrassed to admit he was her lover, she couldn't deny she wanted him.

He managed to unzip his jeans and free himself. She arched upward as he entered her, and his anger fled. He wanted to breathe the smell of her skin, to lose himself in the liquid velvet of her body. He wanted to hold her until she said she loved him. Until she told him she didn't want to see her ex.

Dimly, Will thought he heard Fang bark but he couldn't concentrate on anything but Carolina. Without other warning, the door to the toolroom crashed open and light flooded the area.

Carolina gasped and turned her face into Will's shoulder. They were covered by the sleeping bag, but there could be no doubt as to what they were doing. Will didn't move, he simply leveled a dangerous look toward Brad. In that moment, as far as Will was concerned, Brad was a stranger. "Get the hell out of here."

"That's my sister!"

Carolina made a sound, and Will's arms flexed with the urge to protect her. "Go outside and shut that door," Will warned.

Brad seemed to come to his senses slowly. He turned and slammed the door after him.

Will tried to talk to Carolina, to tell her everything was okay. But she wouldn't look at him. As he withdrew from her, she turned her face to the wall.

Furious at the whole situation, Will stood and pulled on his jeans. He was in the mood to fight. He might as well see what Brad had to say.

He opened the door and stepped outside. A second later, Brad's fist came out of the dark.

"You son-of-a— You just couldn't let one go, could you?" Brad lined himself up to throw another punch.

Will tasted blood, but he wasn't going to fight.

"She's not like the others," he said, moving away from his best friend.

"Yeah, sure!" Brad waded forward for another swing, oblivious to the mismatch. Unconscious of the fact that Will wasn't swinging back.

Will blocked the punch and shoved Brad backward until he stumbled and landed on his butt. "Stay down there while I tell you something!"

Fang circled the two men, barking furiously, but neither paid him any attention. Beyond listening, Brad came up off the floor and tackled Will, sending them both sprawling.

Will was beginning to lose his temper. He pinned Brad beneath him with his body and one forearm on his throat. He wasn't going to hurt Brad, but he'd be damned if he'd let him get in another punch.

Suddenly, light from the doorway spilled around them and Carolina's hands were on Will's shoulders, tugging at him. "Let him go, Will!"

Will responded to the plea in her voice and backed off. He kept a grip on the front of Brad's shirt to make sure he didn't do anything to really make him mad.

As soon as they were standing, Will let go of Brad with a little shove.

Brad turned to Carolina. "I came to your room to apologize for jumping to conclusions. And all along you were—" He couldn't seem to say it. "How could you fall for his line of bull?" He shot a venomous look toward his former best friend before adding, "I thought you were smarter than that."

"Shut up, Brad," Will ordered. He couldn't stand the look on Carolina's face, or the tears running down her cheeks.

"Caro . . ." Will raised one hand to touch her.

She backed away from him and pinned her brother with her gaze. "Brad, I'm a grown woman, capable of making my own decisions." Her voice sounded stronger than she appeared to be at that moment. Will felt a surge of admiration. Then she turned to look at him and said, "And my own mistakes."

Carolina saw Will's jaw tighten as the words hit home. She wanted to scream at him, "This is the truth, this is reality. Everything we've done has been a huge mistake!" But she didn't need to scream. She saw his features close up, saw the anger tighten the muscles in his jaw. The blood on his lip made her want to sob. But she couldn't. She had to be the referee. At that moment she felt like the mother of two little boys.

"Brad, I want you to come back to the cabin with me. Will..." Her voice broke slightly, and she raised her chin to show him she meant business. "I think it's time we all started acting our age." Before she could get away, she was frozen by Will's voice.

"I thought you were acting your age. That you were different. I got the impression that you wanted more than what other women want from me."

Carolina could barely breathe. It was bad enough to hear the derision in Will's voice. She couldn't stand there and listen to it in front of her brother. She gave Brad's arm one determined push toward the cabin and stumbled after him.

12

"LOOK, I KNOW you've been alone for a while. And I know how persuasive Will can be, but—"

"Please, Brad. I don't want to talk about it." Carolina kept her eyes on the road, determined to concentrate on driving. Not on the fact that she was on her way to the airport, on her way to L.A. And she hadn't said goodbye, or anything else, to Will.

"Well, I'm leaving today, too," Brad said with disgust. "I never thought Will would do something like this to me."

Carolina couldn't believe her ears. "What exactly did he do to you?"

"You know, messing around with you. He gave me his word that he wouldn't—" Brad sputtered into an embarrassed silence, as if he was envisioning her and Will together.

Warmth crept into Carolina's face, but she had to keep talking. "This really has nothing to do with you, Brad. It's between Will and me." She chanced a look in her brother's direction. He truly did look upset. Carolina drew in a deep breath. "Don't ruin a friendship that's lasted for years over something that's only lasted a week," she said.

"You don't understand. This is a guy thing. He promised he wouldn't get involved with you in any way. I told him you were still hung up about Paul and—"

"Maybe he helped me," Carolina interrupted.

Brad turned to look at her. "What?"

She hadn't realized the truth until she'd said it. Will had helped her. He'd touched and kissed away the pain of lost trust and broken promises. He'd made her think about love again.

"He helped me realize that maybe I don't want to be alone for the rest of my life. That I might enjoy another relationship sometime in the future."

Brad seemed to consider that for a moment. "You know Will won't be around for any future," he warned.

Will would leave her. She'd known from the beginning that she and Will were temporary. Temporary housemates, temporary co-workers, temporary lovers. A choking clot of fear and doubt seemed to lodge in her throat. She wasn't supposed to care. She wasn't supposed to have fallen in love with him.

"Yes, I know." Carolina knew the pain was coming. But if she stopped to think about it now, she'd fly into a thousand pieces. She only had herself to blame for walking into the same trap as before, for falling in love with a man who would leave. "But he's been good to me. He didn't deserve that punch you gave him."

"He lied to me." Brad's voice heated into anger again. "I asked him point-blank if he'd..." His voice drifted off, as if he couldn't say it.

Carolina's guilt doubled. "He lied because he thought I didn't want you to know."

Brad was silent for a long time.

"At least talk to him about it before you leave." She recovered her big-sister attitude. "And I do mean talk. There's no need for arguments. It's not like you have to defend my virtue or anything." Carolina formed a camouflaging smile. "It's a little late for that."

"Are you going to see Paul when you get to L.A.?"

Carolina's smile faltered. "I don't know." Paul had been far from her thoughts lately. She didn't even remember what she'd said to him on the phone the previous evening.

Carolina made the turnoff toward the airport. She wanted Brad's promise before she got on the plane. "Don't change the subject. Are you going to talk to Will?"

"I don't know. Maybe," Brad echoed her answer, then shrugged like an angry little boy. "All right, all right."

That was something, Carolina decided. If Brad and Will could remain friends, this whole episode wouldn't be a complete disaster. *I got the impression that you wanted more than what other women want from me.* The memory of Will's words the night before tore at Carolina. She pulled the car up to the curb and put it into neutral, feeling as though every drop of blood had been drained from her heart. Running on empty.

THE FIRST FULL DAY of the three-day show was a success. Back in her hotel room, Carolina kicked off her shoes with a weary sigh. She should be satisfied. She'd been busy the entire day and had done well in sales. The time and effort she'd invested into her jewelry designs had paid off. She was good at her work, even if her personal life was teetering on the brink of emotional meltdown.

If she stayed busy, she wouldn't have to think. If she didn't think then the suffocating feeling of loss growing in her heart could be put off a little longer. She couldn't face losing someone else she loved, losing Will. Not yet.

Paul had made an appearance at the show. Carolina glanced at her watch. She'd promised to meet him for dinner in an hour and a half. She wasn't sure why she'd said yes, except for the nagging feeling that she needed to attend to old business. And to stay busy.

She went into the bathroom and twisted the shower faucets on. She glanced at her watch again as she took it off. Maybe she should call Will. No, what they needed to say couldn't be said over the phone. But would he even be there when she got back? She refused to think about that. There was an inevitable ending for them. She couldn't stop it. Carolina swallowed to ease the sadness burning at the back of her throat. If their ending had already happened, then she couldn't stand to know yet.

Stay busy. She pulled her blouse over her head and began to unfasten her hair.

"HEY, MAN, I told you I was sorry," Brad complained. "What's wrong with you, anyhow? I know I didn't hurt you with that punch."

Will just stared at Brad. He felt like shaking him. *It wasn't the punch, you bonehead! It was the look on your sister's face!* "It's not your fault," Will said finally. He didn't know what to blame it on. He just knew that his carefree attitude about life had been blown all to hell. He cared too much, and he didn't want to feel free. And he definitely had an attitude.

"I still don't understand whatever happened between you and Caro. I don't see the attraction. She's at least—"

"Leave it alone, Brad," Will warned. He was beginning to think there were a lot of things his buddy didn't

see. He also hadn't gotten over the fact that Brad
freaked at the thought of him touching his sister.

"I promised Carolina I'd talk to you about this."

Those words stopped Will like he'd hit a wall. He
turned to face his buddy with narrowed eyes and a look
of disbelief. "Carolina wants you to talk to me—about
her and me?"

Brad seemed to backtrack. "Well, not exactly. She
wanted me to apologize."

"I didn't think so." Will watched Brad solemnly. "The
next thing you'll probably do is ask my intentions."

Brad shrugged. "Don't worry. I've known you too
long for that. I know your MO with women. Carolina
knows it, too."

"What are you talking about?" Will's words sounded
as dangerous as he felt.

"She knows whatever's between you is only temporary. She said, 'Don't let something that's lasted a week
wreck a friendship that has lasted for years.'"

A week. Will's entire body tightened. The pain
caused by the finality of that phrase was swift and unexpected. *So she thinks this is it, huh?* his anger countered. Did it have to do with getting a phone call from
her ex?

"Yeah?" Will was suddenly tired of keeping secrets.
"Well, if you remember, I told you that Carolina was
different."

"Of course she's different. She's not even close to
your type. She's—"

"I love her."

Brad's jaw dropped open. Then he laughed. "Bull!
Quit trying to jack me around. You—"

"Love her," Will said again. He hadn't realized the
truth until the words came out of his mouth. He'd been

dancing around the idea for weeks, telling himself that once he'd had enough of her, the fascination would go away. But now he knew he'd never get enough. Now, when it was possibly too late and he had handled everything wrong.

Carolina was mistaken about them being over. Five years before, he'd let Diane go without a fight. What he felt for Carolina was stronger, deeper, more grown-up. He wasn't going to give her up without a war.

THERE WERE LIGHTS twinkling in the trees surrounding the courtyard of the trendy restaurant. Like Christmas in June, Carolina thought as the waiter pulled out a chair for her to be seated. *What in the world am I doing here?* she questioned as Paul seated himself across from her.

"You look very nice tonight," Paul said after the waiter had taken their drink orders and retreated.

Carolina couldn't resist a comeback. "You sound surprised."

When he frowned, she offered him a contrite smile. "Sorry. Let me rephrase that—thank you."

With a self-conscious movement, Paul realigned his tie. Carolina had the sudden blinding insight that he was nervous. The realization should have given her some sense of satisfaction, but she only felt mild surprise. It had been almost a year since they'd been face-to-face. A lot of things in her life had changed in the past year. Even more had changed in the past week.

Carolina's eyes swept over the man she'd spent nearly a third of her life with. His hair had thinned, but not drastically. The frown line on his forehead was etched a little deeper. He was so familiar, and yet a stranger.

"So, how did the first day go?"

Carolina worked to keep the conversation superficial as she filled him in on the jewelry show. Shortly after they'd sat down, she'd realized she had nothing to say to Paul. No unfinished business. Their business had been finished two years before. It was the first pleasant thought she'd had all day.

The waiter came and went with their drinks and dinner order. Then Paul discussed his business plans and an upcoming move to the east coast. The conversation didn't turn personal until dessert was served.

"So, how are you doing, really?" Paul asked.

"Fine," Carolina answered. "Really." She fought his attempt to sway the conversation. "I just told you, business is good. I'm building a new house."

"Are you happy?" Happy? She felt like running out of the restaurant—straight to the airport. Exactly when had Paul ever been worried about her happiness?

"Yes, I'm happy," she lied. *I'm ecstatic! I've fallen in love when I didn't want to. I've hurt the last person I ever wanted to hurt—Will. And I'm not sure how I'll survive one more goodbye. Other than that, I'm terrific.* She hoped she had a happy look on her face to go along with the lie. She'd swallow her fork before she'd tell him anything about Will.

"I know you're going to say I told you so," Paul began without questioning her further. "But Heather and I have split up."

He'd seriously surprised her. He looked ready to pour his heart out. Carolina put down her fork, stalling for time. She didn't want to hear this. What did he expect her to say? She'd never said I told you so in her life.

"I'm sorry," she managed.

Paul looked at her for a long time. "It's hard for me to admit, but you might have been right about younger women."

With an incredulous laugh, Carolina raised one hand to stop his speech. "Me? Right? If I remember correctly, nobody ever asked my opinion." *This is your fault, not mine*, she wanted to say. "Did it ever occur to you that you might have been wrong about younger women?"

Paul stared at her dumbfounded.

"LET'S GO OUT and get drunk, like the good old days," Brad said.

Will studied his watch. Seven-thirty, L.A. time. Would Carolina be back from the show yet? At that moment, he couldn't remember anything good about the old days. He wanted to talk to Carolina. Now.

"Where's the number for Carolina's hotel?"

Brad dug through the papers stuck in his wallet. "She probably won't be there," he grumbled. "I've never seen you act so weird about a woman since that thing with Diane." He handed the piece of paper to Will. "You know Caro's ex-husband lives in L.A. She's probably out with him."

Will silenced Brad with a hostile look, then snatched the card from his hand and dialed the number. When the hotel operator answered, he asked for Carolina Villada. It was then the hammer of realization hit him. Carolina still used her ex-husband's name. If she didn't care about him anymore, why did she keep his name?

The phone rang seven times before the operator broke in and asked if he'd like to leave a message.

"No, no message," Will said and hung up the phone, but his heart was pumping too fast in his chest. And his mind kept repeating, *Come home, Carolina. Come home to me.*

PAUL HELD the passenger door of his Lexus open for Carolina. She'd taken a cab to the restaurant, and he'd insisted on dropping her at her hotel.

"You really have changed," Paul said, looking at her as if he was seeing her for the first time. "You must be happy. You seem a lot stronger than I remember."

Trapped between the car door and her ex-husband's bemused expression, Carolina smiled. It was quite a compliment, coming from the man who'd tested every measure of strength she owned. "Yes, I have changed." Thank God. But was she strong enough to survive losing Will?

"You know," he said, seeming to choose his words with care. "This new job is in Connecticut. Do you remember that old house we looked at before? The one you wanted to redo?"

Carolina nodded but withheld comment. The memory seemed like a dream from another lifetime. She had another house now, and another man to help build it.

"If you were interested in trying again, maybe this time we could—"

"Paul." Carolina had to stop him. Two years ago she would have bartered her soul to hear those words. Now they just made her sad. There was no point in allowing Paul to think she would even consider getting back together with him. She had her own life, her work, her new house. And Will . . . for one night at a time. Unless the last night they were together had changed his mind. She touched Paul's hand, which rested on the car door. "I'm sorry."

Paul shrugged and sighed. "Yeah. I know." He moved out of her path and shut the car door after her.

Carolina turned and gave him a brief hug. "Take care."

"You, too," Paul said as he returned her embrace. And it almost sounded like he meant it.

AFTER THE TWELFTH RING, Carolina hung up the phone. No answer at the cabin. She wondered if Will and Brad really had killed each other. Or had they both left Arizona for parts unknown? She flopped down on the bed and stared at the empty black screen of the television set. There was no way she'd ever be able to sleep. She had to talk to Will, to hear his voice.

She had to know if he'd be there when she got back. Her fears had squeezed through the tiny silence between the rings of the phone like a stampede of crazed horses trapped in a narrow canyon.

And now they were running wild.

Where was he? Carolina picked up the phone and dialed the number of the cabin again. *Don't go, Will. Not yet.*

WILL LEANED BACK and nursed his beer as he watched Brad try to talk a young blond cocktail waitress out of the lacy garter she was wearing. He didn't like this bar much.

The Coyote Club. The name seemed to say it all. The customers were barely legal, the music was about two decibels too loud and . . . he had a headache. He wistfully thought of the Square Peg Tavern, but that only brought back memories of Carolina in his arms on the dance floor.

He frowned and took another swig of beer. Maybe he should leave. His hand tightened on the beer bottle at the thought of going back to the empty cabin.

Where was Carolina?

He hadn't meant what he said to her the night before. He couldn't really believe she was using him. That she didn't care at least a little. But he'd had to watch her walk away. Then she'd run to L.A. without a word. Had she run to her ex-husband? Like Diane?

Will ran a hand over his face. He'd sworn he'd never do this again. That he'd never give another woman the opportunity to get close enough to hurt him. And most women didn't mind. They only wanted what he could do for them, or *to* them. Carolina had somehow slipped under his guard. He'd thought he was in control of everything—business as usual. Until he'd seen that look on her face after Brad had punched him. It was then he realized he loved her, and instead of holding her and comforting her—and confessing the truth—he'd let her walk away.

Because the pained look on her face and the words she'd said had nearly killed him. Damn. He knew he ought to leave. Just disappear. And let the whole episode expire from lack of participation. He'd done that so many times before. But he knew he was too far gone this time. Carolina would have to look him in the eye and tell him to hit the road. The very real possibility that she'd do just that made his chest hurt.

He wasn't going to call her again. He'd wait. When she came home, when he could look into her honey-colored eyes, he'd tell her the truth. Then he'd leave, if that's what she wanted.

"I NEED TO TALK to Will," Carolina said.

"He's over at the new house with the crew," Brad informed her. "I came over to grab a bite to eat."

"Go get him, Brad. Please. I'll call back in fifteen minutes."

"All right. But he's as cranky as a bear."

Carolina sighed, and a little of the tension eased out of her muscles. Will was at the house, still working. Cranky or not, she could talk to him in the next few minutes.

"Hey, are you okay?" Brad sounded concerned.

"No," she answered truthfully. "But I've been worse." Like last night, her mind added. When she couldn't sleep, couldn't dream, couldn't think about anything but Will. "Go get him. I'll call back."

Carolina waited about twelve minutes—close enough. She'd tried to rehearse something to say, but since she'd been the one who walked away from him and she didn't know how he felt about it, the best she could come up with was, I'm sorry.

The phone rang twice before Will picked it up.

"Hello." There was no question behind the greeting, merely an opening. Instead of feeling relieved, Carolina's pulse went off the scale.

"Will?"

"Yeah?" She could hear him breathing. She had to rush on before the silence killed her courage.

"I'm so sorry." Despite her best effort, her voice wobbled. "I should have never lied to Brad about us. If I'd been honest, none of this would have happened."

"Caro . . ." Will formed her name like a loving curse. She could envision him impatiently shoving one hand through his hair. "I don't even know what happened or who should be sorry. I . . . When are you coming home?"

Carolina closed her eyes. "Tomorrow. As soon as I can."

"Everything will be okay." She couldn't tell if he was soothing her or himself. "Just come home. I'll be at the airport."

"All right." She held on to the phone because even though she'd run out of words, she didn't want to say goodbye.

"Carolina?"

"Hmm?"

"Thanks for calling."

IT SEEMED to take forever for the passengers to move up the aisle. Carolina stood, loaded down with her carry-on bags, squashed between two insurance salesmen, and tried to calm the pounding of her heart. Just a few more moments, a few more feet and she would be off this plane. And she would be with Will. Finally, people in the crowded aisle began to shift and move. Carolina could breathe again as she walked down the jetway and into the terminal.

Will was difficult to miss, standing a head taller than most of the people around him, including Brad. Carolina had to remind herself to keep breathing, keep walking.

"Hi," she said, coming to a stop in front of them. She wanted to throw her arms around Will and laugh. To tell him that the last three days had been hell. Instead, she just stood there staring at him stupidly.

Will automatically reached to relieve her of her bags. After setting them at his feet, he pulled her into his arms. Exactly where she wanted to be.

"Hi," he said into her ear. She felt a slight tremor run through his muscles as he tightened his grip. Surrounded by the warm, solid strength of his body, Carolina breathed in the smell of him and experienced a singing note of pure joy. He was glad to see her.

"My plane leaves in thirty minutes," Brad announced.

Will's embrace shifted slowly, as if he would let go but only when he was damned good and ready. Carolina turned to face her brother and almost laughed. He looked like an eight-year-old being forced to watch the mushy parts of a movie. Gross. Why had she ever been worried about what Brad thought of her and Will?

"Are you two friends again?" she asked.

"Yeah. We're okay. Right?" Brad looked at Will. Will nodded.

"I leave out of gate seven," Brad continued.

Will motioned for Carolina to follow her brother, then picked up her bags and fell into step alongside her.

His actions seemed to say, first things first. They would get Brad to his gate, then they would be alone.

THEY MADE IT as far as the parking lot of the airport before Will knew he couldn't wait any longer to kiss her. He tossed her bags into the back of his truck and dragged her to him. He wanted to say he was sorry but he didn't even know what he'd done. He wanted to tell her he'd fallen in love. But he ended up with his face pushed into her hair, choking on the words. So he let his lips do the talking, and his hands. The hot desert sun had nothing on the heat that seemed to be moving under his skin.

Carolina's mouth opened under his, and the very air seemed to shudder. Her body pressed close, offering, asking. And Will knew the answer to that question.

"I missed you," he admitted in a rush after kissing them both to the brink.

"I missed you, too." Her breath was moist and warm along his neck. Will closed his eyes. He didn't want to change the subject, to spoil the moment, but he knew they had to get some things straight.

"We need to talk," he said.

She nodded, but didn't let go of him. Someone beeped a car horn a few rows over in the lot. The sound set Will into motion. He guided Carolina to the truck and opened the door. The sooner they got on the road, the sooner they'd be home. The sooner they talked, the sooner they could make love.

It was an hour and a half drive to Prescott. Now that Will finally had Carolina's undivided attention, he wasn't sure how to start.

"Are you still worried about Brad?" he asked.

"No. And for the life of me I don't know why I got so upset." She drew one knee under her on the seat and turned to watch him drive. "Actually, I do know why. It's just hard to say it." She paused. "I couldn't admit we were lovers because I didn't want people to think I was doing the same thing my husband did. Paul divorced me for a younger woman, and I..." She seemed to run out of words. "I couldn't believe that a young guy like you would be attracted to me." Her gaze drifted to the horizon. "There are so many other, younger women out there. And then when we did...make love—" Tears rose in her eyes and spilled over.

It was all Will could do to keep the truck on the road. He wanted to hold her, but he also wanted her to talk.

She turned and looked at him steadily, without bothering to wipe away the tears on her face. "Getting what you want is almost as scary as the thought of losing it."

Will couldn't take those tears. They were like acid on his heart. He slowed the truck and reached across her to the glove compartment. Without taking his eyes off the road, he reached inside for a clean bandanna to give her. As he pulled it, something else fell out and landed on the floorboard next to her foot. Carolina bent to retrieve the object, and Will glanced over to see what had fallen.

A red and white lace garter with a tiny buckle that read, Coyote Club. Will remembered Brad spinning it around his finger as they'd left the bar two nights before.

The stunned expression on Carolina's face cut through him like a chain saw. All the color seemed to drain out of her. With the movements of a robot on automatic pilot, she put the garter into the glove compartment and gently shut the cover. Then she said, "Stop the truck."

He could barely hear her words over the thunder of his heartbeat in his ears. They were twenty minutes away from anything that could be mistaken for a town. He slowed the truck, preparing to pull into a roadside rest stop, while his brain was screaming, *Do something! Say something!*

The rest stop consisted of a concrete table with a covering for shade, two garbage cans and a lot of rocks. Will brought the truck to a halt, and before the dust settled, he was out the door and around the truck. Carolina had already shoved open the passenger door and stumbled away.

She was afraid she was going to be sick. Humiliation rose in her throat, causing her stomach to heave. God. How could she have been such a fool? Here she was, pouring her heart out to him and he—

"Carolina?" She felt his touch on her arm and flinched. She didn't want to touch him, couldn't look at him.

"For once in my life, I have to admit my brother was right," she gasped between deep breaths. "He said you always find a woman." She clamped her arms over her stomach to keep from falling down. To keep from raising her face to the sky and wailing like a wild woman. How many times did she have to learn this lesson?

"I was convenient until I had to go to L.A., and then you found someone else who was more convenient."

"That's not what happened. It belongs to Brad. You can ask him."

"I called and you weren't home," she accused and then wished she hadn't told him. Poor Carolina, worrying and phoning while he was out having a good time.

Will stared at the braided strands in Carolina's hair, alternating between frustration at the misunderstanding and anger that she'd assumed the worst. She didn't believe him. Wasn't going to listen to him.

"Caro." Will grasped her arm and turned her around. He started to pull her toward him, but she shook her head to halt his progress.

"Just stay away from me."

"No." Will's anger kicked into high gear. "And while we're on the subject of calling, what about your ex-husband? Did you see him?" The words were out of his mouth before he could weigh the consequences.

She looked shocked, but didn't deny anything. Will felt like he'd been blindsided, yet his mouth kept moving. "I called your hotel. I called to—"

"Yes, I saw him."

Will carefully brought both his hands up to smooth his hair as if he could sweep her answer out of his mind. "Dammit! I didn't want to know that." He turned and walked a few steps in the direction the truck was headed.

The hissing sound of a car rolling by on the roadway filled the silence between them. Will felt so odd, as if he'd been sucker punched or had bumped his head too hard. His gaze locked on the hazy, distant point where the road seemed to plunge off the edge of the earth, and the truth came tumbling out.

"I called to tell you that I love you."

He blinked once, surprised he'd actually said the words out loud. Then Carolina was standing in front of him. "Will, how can you say that when you were with another woman last night or the night before?" She looked ready to cry again. "I don't need to hear a bunch of pretty words and promises. All I want is the truth."

She didn't believe him. What was he supposed to think about that? He'd only told one other woman he loved her. And he meant it more this time.

"It is the truth. I love you, and I haven't been with any other women." He wished she would tell him that she loved him, too. But she didn't. "Do you actually think that after weeks of hardly being able to keep my hands off you I would look for another woman because you were out of sight for two days?"

Carolina brought one hand up as if to rub a pain out of her forehead. "No. Collecting garters is more Brad's style. It's just that I—"

"What about your ex? Is he what this is really all about?"

"No, this is about us. You and me," she answered in a sure tone. "I saw Paul and we talked. But he's not part of my life anymore, and that's the way I want it."

She didn't resist when he encircled her in his arms. "I know you don't want to get involved with any-one...that your plans don't include me." He rocked her gently back and forth. "But I want...I *need* to be with you." She started to speak, but he cut her off in case she was about to say no. "Just until the house is finished, if that's what you want. Please." He lowered his mouth closer to hers. "You know I can make it good for you."

The truth. I love you. She loved him enough to wish with all her heart that she could believe him. But the truth was, even the fact that he believed he loved her couldn't make it true. What could a man like Will know about love and commitment? About sticking around when circumstances or people changed? He'd never settled in one place or stuck with one person long enough to find out. And he couldn't make her believe he'd stay with her.

But she wanted to love him, if only while she could have him. "I do care about you," she whispered, al-most afraid to say it too loud. She brought one hand up to trace the hard plane of his jaw and looked into his unwavering gaze. He looked like he was holding his breath. "But I don't know what to do about it," she confessed.

"Just don't run away from it." She felt, more than saw, his throat muscles tighten as he swallowed. "Or from me," he added.

The irony of his words clawed at Carolina's heart. *I'm not a runner,* she wanted to say. *You know exactly where I'll be for the next twenty years or so—in my house. But where will you be?*

"Let's go home," she said, unwilling and unable to think about that inevitable part—the future.

13

WILL LEANED against a tree and watched Carolina lug a basket of wet laundry out to the clothesline. Fang followed close on her heels as if he'd been invited to a party.

Hanging clothes, such an old-fashioned thing. Carolina was definitely a motivated woman with her own life, her own career. But some things were timeless, ageless. The past few weeks had taught him that. When Carolina gracefully bent to pull one of his shirts from the basket, Will knew he wanted to stay right where he was, to watch Carolina, to love her. For a long, long time.

The house was ready for the final touches—furniture, rugs, people. He wondered if Carolina had considered the possibility of him staying, of making this temporary arrangement permanent. Hell, he'd almost blurted it out the night before. He'd almost said the M word. After they'd made love, after she'd...nearly given him a heart attack. His body reacted to the memory of her mouth on him, her legs straddling his hips.

She'd never said she loved him. He was still waiting for those words and all they implied. He could feel it in her touch, see it in her eyes. But he needed to hear it before he put his heart on the line and asked for more.

Through a distracted daze Will saw Carolina pull one of his red bandannas from the basket. Fang came to attention as if the material belonged exclusively to him.

Carolina pointed a finger at the dog with a look that said, "Don't even think about it."

Will's heart seemed to rise and expand in his chest. He realized he was happy. With a laugh, he pushed away from the tree and walked toward them, thinking he could definitely get to like it around here. He gave a short whistle, causing both Fang and Carolina to look in his direction before he waved.

That's when he saw the mail truck pulling up past the cabin. The carrier got out and called to Carolina. By the time Will reached her, she was holding an overnight delivery letter in her hand.

"It's for you," Carolina said, handing it over. She watched the puzzled look on Will's face change to one of comprehension.

"It's from my sister. What in the world is she sending me that couldn't come by regular . . ." He tore open the cardboard and pulled out another, well-traveled envelope. Carolina could see foreign postage stamps and at least three different addresses where the letter had been forwarded, then forwarded again. Unreasonable dread swamped her, and she held her breath. Please, be good news, she chanted silently.

Will pried open the envelope, quickly scanned the message inside, then laughed. "It's from the Tashimo company in Tokyo." Judging by his smile, Carolina decided he must have won the Arizona lottery. "Great news," he nearly shouted. "They're inviting me to Japan, to work on the Shinto temple."

GREAT NEWS. Carolina picked up a polishing rag and went to work on a finished piece of silver. She had to stay busy, stay focused. She had to work. That's all she needed, wasn't it? Her work? Her new house? Tears filled her eyes and blurred her vision, but she kept polishing. Hadn't she known this day would come? The feel of the cool silver in her hands calmed her, centered her. She could deal with this, her mind countered, as the pain in her heart continued to squeeze tears from her eyes.

The tinkle of the bell on the studio door sounded dull. Carolina tried to sniff back her tears. She was caught. Her hands were too dirty to wipe her face.

Will swiveled her chair around in his direction and chucked her chin up. Without saying a word, he removed her glasses and rubbed away her tears with the pads of his thumbs. Then he bent down and kissed her.

"We need to talk."

Carolina abandoned the polishing cloth and waited. She wanted to close her eyes and block out the distress in Will's gaze, but she couldn't ignore reality. It was time to face the real world.

"I don't want to leave," Will said.

Carolina drew in a fortifying breath. "You have to," she replied. She needed to be adult about this. She could cry later. "I've known that all along."

"No." Will frowned at her. "I don't have to."

"Will, you've waited a long time for this opportunity. You can't just blow it off because . . ."

"I can do anything I want. We can do anything we want." He gripped one of her hands. "Why don't you come with me?" Will squatted to look into her eyes. "We could get married."

Sadness nearly choked Carolina. Married. She shook her head. She had learned the hard way that vows and love couldn't hold someone determined to go. She reclaimed her hand and stood up, forcing Will to do the same. "No."

Suddenly his hands were on her shoulders. "I wanted to ask you before the letter came. I wanted to stay before this came up, because I love you."

"No, Will." Carolina pulled away and turned her back to him before he could kiss her, before he could convince her that they could do anything. She wanted to put her hands over her ears to stop his words. She wanted to beg him to stay. She squeezed her eyes shut instead. He'd convinced her of so much already—passion, love. But she couldn't gamble on another shaky future. A future with two strikes against it already. Carolina faced him once more in order to tell him the truth. "I do love you."

His expression changed at the sound of her words. She continued before he could interrupt. "But I won't go with you, and I won't ask you to stay. You know you'll never be happy in one place. You have your dreams and you should go after them."

"*Bull!* We're not talking about dreams here. We're talking about real things, important things. You say you love me." He stepped toward her until she had to raise her chin in order to look him in the eyes. "Maybe I want you—and I want to work in Japan for six months. It's not so hard to figure out how to make that happen." He gave her a hard, exasperated look. "But you're too busy saying 'I won't' because of what your ex-husband did."

"You don't understand."

"No," he snapped. "I don't. You're saying it doesn't matter if I stay or go. Because of what happened in the past, there's no chance for us. You'd rather hide out here than have a life with me."

Carolina's anger kicked into gear. "If you want a woman without a past, then find someone younger. Someone your own age who doesn't know that love can't fix everything. I put aside my dreams for years and followed a man from promotion to promotion, all in the name of love. Then one day, love left and Paul went on without me. I'll never be fooled by that fairy tale again. I made a change in my life because I had to. It was the only way to survive." Her eyes were filling with tears, and that made her even madder. "You say you love me, but what about a year from now, or ten years from now? When I have a few more wrinkles or some gray in my hair. When you decide that working anywhere is preferable to staying here with *me!*" She ended on a strident note, and her tears spilled over.

Time to say goodbye. Better to do it now than later. Carolina drew in a cleansing breath to get her through the devastation of the next moment of her life. "I've known from the beginning that you'd leave. It's better that you do it now."

CAROLINA WATCHED the men moving in and out the front door of her new home and felt very little excitement or joy.

Will was leaving. She could see him across the yard talking to the man in charge of the moving crew. In the last two days they'd barely spoken. She'd packed her belongings, then unpacked them in the new house. Will had packed his belongings and tossed them into the back of his truck along with his tools and now Fang. They had come full circle—strangers again.

She could do this. It hurt, but this was the best way, the only way. She'd spent every waking hour reminding herself that she wasn't a foolish girl anymore. Every extra moment remembering the hard lessons she'd learned, and each flashing second focusing on doing the safe thing for her life, for her heart. What kind of idiot made the same mistake twice?

But knowing Will hadn't been a mistake. As she watched him walk toward her, something inside her chest went haywire. *Don't let him go. Tell him you want him, no matter what happens, no matter how long it lasts.*

"Well, that's it," Will said, unable to prolong his leaving for very much longer. He brushed his palms together, then slid his hands into his back pockets to keep from touching Carolina. He wanted to smile, to show her he could walk away like a grown-up—without a scene—but he hadn't been able to smile for the past few days. He was beginning to believe that she was really going to let him walk out of her life, and the reality of that twisted in his gut like barbed wire. "You'll be able to sleep in your new house tonight."

Carolina stared at him without speaking. The urge to shake that complacent look off her face contracted the muscles in his arms. "You can send the final check to my sister's address," he said unnecessarily. She'd offered to pay him before he left, but he couldn't stand the thought of getting money tangled up with goodbye.

"Carolina . . ." He sighed and looked away, toward his truck. How in the hell was he going to leave her?

"Goodbye, Will." She extended one hand to shake his, as if they were what they'd started out to be—employee, employer. But her wide amber eyes looked empty, and the sight made this goodbye all too real.

Will stared at her hand, remembering her fingers running over his skin, knowing that if he touched her, he'd yank her into his arms. And that was the one place he knew she didn't want to be.

Goodbye. He couldn't say it. He turned and forced one foot in front of the other until he reached the truck and Fang. Until he stood on the threshold of the first day of the rest of his life, without Carolina.

THE SILENCE was killing her. Carolina sighed and leaned her head back to rest against the chair. She'd spent the day in her studio, working until her eyes felt permanently crossed. Now she wanted to relax on the porch of her new home and wait for twilight. But instead of soothing, the silent woods surrounding her house seemed empty, deserted. Like the rooms of her old cabin. Like the desolate, too-loud echo of her own heartbeat.

Alone. She hadn't seen or spoken to another human being for three days. That had to be a new personal record. Complete solitude. What once would have seemed like heaven was quickly turning out to be hell. She decided to make a wind chime to hang on the porch—a cheerful sound to keep her company. That would take care of the silence.

She hadn't heard a word from Will. He'd walked away from her eleven days before without looking back—just like she'd wanted him to do. And now, silence.

Carolina pushed out of the heavy wooden chair. She had to do something! She couldn't sit and think about Will. She paced to the front door of her house, reached for the doorknob, then stopped. Going inside would only make it worse. Everywhere she turned there were reminders of Will. His shadow seemed to fall on her every step, and his touch remained in every wonderful thing he had built for her.

She missed the man she loved. What was he doing? Was he safely in Japan? Did he think about her at all? Carolina jerked the door open. *You can do this*, her mind repeated. *You're an adult, capable of taking care of yourself. You have your own life, your own dreams.* The room, with its warm welcome and gorgeous, panoramic view of the valley, seemed to swim before her eyes. Her heart couldn't see the merits of the solitary life of a capable adult. Her heart wanted Will.

Slowly, she made her way up the stairs to her bedroom. She curled up on her bed and thanked the maker of all things that she and Will had never made love in her new bedroom. It was the one place she could feel truly alone.

"I THINK I'm going crazy," Carolina confessed.

"Again?" Sue Ann sat back in her chair and studied her friend, but she didn't laugh.

Carolina's eyes filled with tears. "You see?" She sniffed, infuriated. "I can't seem to get through a day without crying. I hate this!" She pulled a tissue out of her pocket and angrily wiped her cheeks. "I don't know how people manage when they..."

"When they fall in love?"

Carolina stared at Sue Ann for a few silent seconds. Then she shut her eyes and sighed. "Yes." She balanced her elbows on the table and cradled her forehead in her hands. "I wasn't supposed to love him, or miss him." She looked up at her friend, allowing all her misery to show. "I even miss his deranged dog." The shrill whistle of the teakettle interrupted. "And now—" Carolina got to her feet "—I can hardly stand to be out here alone."

As she walked into the kitchen and took the kettle from the burner, Sue Ann said, "You're not crazy, you've just changed."

"Great," Carolina grumped when she returned with tea. "I was perfectly fine until Will came along."

"No, you weren't," Sue Ann interrupted. "You were hiding in your cabin, in the woods." She frowned as she stirred her tea. "Somebody needed to come along to change that. I'm just sorry it was someone who wouldn't stay."

"He wanted to stay," Carolina managed. "I wouldn't let him."

"Oh, Caro..."

"TELL THEM I can stay for as long as they need me," Will said into the phone. Yeah, he was a free man. Nothing holding him on this side of the Pacific. Damn. He'd been totally at odds with the world in general for the past eleven days, and he was having a difficult time forcing a normal sound into his voice.

But he wanted the job, didn't he? Wasn't it his one aim in life to be on that plane to Tokyo at the end of the week?

"Give me a call when they know specifics. You know where to find me." He hung up the phone.

Carolina knew where to find him, too. He'd thought for sure he would have heard from her by now. That she'd call and at least say... What? She'd said goodbye. Sent his check. How many times did he need to hear it before he believed it?

Damn. Damn. *Damn.*

He looked at the phone. He knew her number. All he had to do was pick up the receiver and punch a few buttons. And say what? How can you survive without me? How can you live inside my skin for months and then say so long when the job is done?

How many times had he done just that? Said so long and walked away? He rubbed his face with one hand, wishing he could scour her memory out of his mind, out of his body. Out of his heart. Damn. Not with Carolina. How in the hell was he going to leave her when he knew they were better off together? When he knew if they both tried, they could do anything, as long as they were together.

Will walked to the window overlooking the front yard of his sister's house. Outside, Fang was involved in a tug-of-war with Jeanne's oldest boy over a knotted pair of socks. Will felt each pull as if it was his heart in the dog's teeth, being yanked in two directions. Maybe he'd take a drive—he glanced at his beat-up truck—too much noise around this house, too many people. He needed to be alone. But he hesitated. If he got in his truck, he was liable to keep on driving until he reached Carolina's front door. The front door of the house he'd built with his hands . . . and with his heart. Damn.

CAROLINA DREW her knees up and rested her chin on her crossed arms. The view from the rocks hadn't changed. But she felt different. It had been exactly three weeks since she'd last seen Will, and the grief inside her had finally eased a little. Tears came less often. She was able to breathe again, as long as she didn't think. As long as she didn't probe too deeply into what could have been different.

Will had to be in Japan by now, and knowing he was completely out of reach was somehow easier to bear. There were no more decisions to make, questions to answer. She didn't have the option of breaking down and calling him, pleading with him to come back. She had no idea how to reach him. Now she could concentrate on getting through each day until the pain went away. Until her heart healed.

You should have gone with him. Sue Ann's words haunted her. Her friend could never understand. Following a man. It sounded so romantic. Carolina had played that game before and been a loser. She wasn't going to volunteer for the pain again.

Will was not like Paul. That was one point Carolina would concede. Will wasn't like Paul, or like Brad. He was his own man. A man who dealt with life on one-to-one terms like he built houses. She knew she'd never meet anyone like him again.

But Will needed his dreams, his own goals. Just because she loved him didn't mean she had the right to ask him to give up his way of life. Just because he said he loved her didn't mean he wouldn't leave her some day.

You should have gone with him. Carolina gritted her teeth. Even if she had gone, it would only have prolonged the time until they had to say goodbye.

Carolina's eyes were open, but her mind was filled with memories of hearing Will's laugh, of watching him work. Of being in his arms. The sound of a car rumbling down the road to her cabin intruded on the silence around her. Carolina was too lost in her memories to worry about someone taking the wrong turn.

She could have gone with Will. She could have been with him, loved him, for at least six more months. And she'd said no. Because she wanted more than six months. She wanted all or nothing.

The silence of the surrounding trees seemed to mock her. *You've got nothing now. If you hadn't been so busy saying no, you and Will might have—* Silence. The part of her mind in charge of self-preservation interrupted with a news flash. The vehicle that had driven by on the road to her old cabin hadn't turned around, as she'd assumed. It had stopped.

Carolina heard a rustling sound, as if something was sprinting through the trees. The skin on the back of her neck tingled, and for the first time in the two and a half years she'd lived alone, she felt uneasy. She decided that she'd meet whatever or whoever it was on solid ground and began to climb down the rocks.

As she reached the bottom, she turned in time to receive the full force of a furry flying body—a dog with a red bandanna tied around his neck.

"Fang, come."

Will... Carolina couldn't even say his name out loud, she was so afraid that she was having a dream or a hallucination. Maybe she finally had gone crazy. But Fang's joyous, slobbered greeting was real. And Will was walking along the trail toward her, tall and solid. He'd come back.

He faced her like a gunfighter primed for the showdown of his life. "Don't say anything, just listen." Will was determined to make his speech before Carolina recovered from the shock of his arrival. She was glad to see him, he could tell that much. But he needed to keep her off balance until he could somehow convince her that they should be together. He looked her over from head to toe. God, he'd missed her. She'd have to have him arrested, dragged away. He'd show her just how immature he could be.

"I got all the way to the airport in San Francisco," he said, then hesitated. *Ask her!* his mind demanded, *before she sees you're scared to death that she'll say no again.* "I told them I couldn't make the trip—that I had a wedding to go to."

The undisguised look of pain in her brown eyes hit him like the arc from a stun gun. He forgot his speech and put his soul on the line.

"Marry me."

"Will . . ."

"I know you don't think I'll stick around," he said, before she could say it. "And I don't have any guarantees about the future." He stared into her eyes, willing her to believe in him. "But I love you and I've had a lot of time to think about this, about us. About what I want. I've decided I don't need to go halfway around the world to build something sacred or spiritual. I want to stay here and build something that will last, with you."

Tears glittered in Carolina's eyes. Whether she said yes or no, Will had to touch her. He wrapped his fingers around her upper arms to steady them both, but he didn't draw her close. "I swear to God that no matter where I have to work, I'll come back here," he pledged. "I'll always need to come back." His chest was so tight he could hardly breathe. "This is my home, too."

Carolina blinked at the tears making wet trails down her face. "You have no idea how badly I want to believe that," she whispered.

Will closed his eyes and swore under his breath. "How can I prove it to you?" He searched her face, demanding some clue. "Carolina, I've been with a lot of women, a lot of younger women. But I never asked any of them to marry me. I never needed them or loved them like I do you. As far as forever is concerned, I'm the only guarantee I can offer."

Guarantee. Would that do it? Written in stone, till death do us part? That's what marriage was all about—not a guarantee but a commitment to try to make a life. Together. Paul had broken his commitment to her. But Will was so very different from Paul. Will had fulfilled every promise he'd ever made her, and then some. And now he was standing in front of her willing to make more. Carolina searched inside, digging around for the fear, for the disbelief. But she only felt her heart beating faster, with love and with excitement for the promise of the future. The future with Will.

"Could we make the trip our honeymoon?"

Will looked like he was afraid to believe his ears. "Does that mean you'll marry me *and* go to Japan?"

She stepped closer and twined her arms around him. "What sane woman would pass up the opportunity to spend a few months in an exotic country with the man she loves?" She pressed her forehead to his chest. Her voice was muffled but the words were clear. "I don't want to be alone anymore. I want to be with you."

Will laughed, then wrapped his arms tight around the woman he loved, lifted her from the ground and spun in a circle. He felt like shouting or dancing . . . or making love.

Fang ran in a wider circle around them, barking, as Will found Carolina's mouth with his own. After one long, mind-numbing kiss, Carolina drew back. The sparkling happiness in her honey eyes and the playful angle of her mouth made Will's heartbeat jump. She poked one insistent finger into the center of his chest to make her point. "But the dog has to stay outside."

4 new short romances all wrapped up in 1 sparkling volume.

Join four delightful couples as they journey home for the festive season—and discover the true meaning of Christmas...that love is the best gift of all!

A Man To Live For - Emma Richmond

Yule Tide - Catherine George

Mistletoe Kisses - Lynsey Stevens

Christmas Charade - Kay Gregory

Available: November 1995   **Price: £4.99**

MILLS & BOON

MILLS & BOON

CHRISTMAS CRACKERS

A cracker of a gift pack full of
Mills & Boon goodies. You'll find...

Passion—in *A Savage Betrayal* by Lynne Graham
A beautiful baby—in *A Baby for Christmas* by Anne McAllister
A Yuletide wedding—in *Yuletide Bride* by Mary Lyons
A Christmas reunion—in *Christmas Angel* by Shannon Waverly

Special Christmas price of 4 books
for £5.99 (usual price £7.96)

Published: November 1995

This month's irresistible novels from

Temptation

IN PRAISE OF YOUNGER MEN by Lyn Ellis

Will Case was too big, far too attractive and much, much too sexy. And for the next few months, he would be sharing a cabin with Carolina. Will was also best friends with her little brother—and the same age!

THE RELUCTANT HUNK by Lorna Michaels

Ariel Foster wanted Jeff McBride to do a series for her TV station. She knew every woman in town would tune in to watch the drop-dead gorgeous man, if only she could persuade him to work for her. But she soon realised she wanted the reluctant hunk for herself.

BACHELOR HUSBAND by Kate Hoffmann

Come live and love in L.A. with the tenants of Bachelors Arms. The first in a captivating new mini-series.

Tru Hallihan lives in this trendy apartment block and has no thoughts of settling down. But he can't resist a bet to date popular radio presenter, Caroline Leighton. Caroline will only co-operate at a price—Tru must pose as her husband for a day!

SECOND-HAND BRIDE by Roseanne Williams

Brynn had married Flint Wilder knowing he was on the rebound from her twin sister, Laurel. Six months later, Brynn had left Flint, fearing she'd never be more than a substitute for her twin. Now Brynn was back in town and Flint seemed hell-bent on making up. But could she ever be sure she wasn't just a stand-in for her sister?

Spoil yourself next month
with these four novels from

THE TWELVE GIFTS OF CHRISTMAS
by Rita Clay Estrada

Pete Cade might be the hunk every woman dreams of finding
under her tree, but he wasn't ready to give the special gift at
the top of Carly Michaels's Christmas list—a father for her
daughter.

THE STRONG SILENT TYPE by Kate Hoffmann

*Come live and love in L.A. with the tenants of Bachelors Arms.
Second in a captivating mini-series.*

Strong and silent Josh Banks had never been the subject of
gossip before. But suddenly everyone was warning him about
wild women—ever since he'd promised to keep party girl
Taryn Wilde out of trouble. He could handle her...couldn't he?

FANCY-FREE by Carrie Alexander

Some residents don't approve of newcomer Fancy O'Brien
taking a bath—in town—to publicize the opening of her bath
boutique. But Jeremiah Quick is glad Fancy has arrived. He
thinks Fancy's the right woman for him. Too bad *Fancy* thinks
he's the right man for her mother...

BARGAIN BASEMENT BABY by Leandra Logan

Marriage had never appealed to Greg Baron. But since he was
going to be a father, he didn't have much choice. If only the
Baron family wasn't so thrilled to finally have an heir. If only
his image of Jane Haley pregnant wasn't so delectable...

Return this coupon and we'll send you 4 Temptations and a mystery gift absolutely FREE! We'll even pay the postage and packing for you.

We're making you this offer to introduce you to the benefits of Reader Service: FREE home delivery of brand-new Temptations, at least a month before they are available in the shops, FREE gifts and a monthly Newsletter packed with information.

Accepting these FREE books and gift places you under no obligation to buy, you may cancel at any time, even after receiving just your free shipment. Simply complete the coupon below and send it to:

MILLS & BOON READER SERVICE, FREEPOST, CROYDON, SURREY, CR9 3WZ.

No stamp needed

Yes, please send me 4 free Temptations and a mystery gift. I understand that unless you hear from me, I will receive 4 superb new titles every month for just £1.99* each postage and packing free. I am under no obligation to purchase any books and I may cancel or suspend my subscription at any time, but the free books and gifts will be mine to keep in any case. (I am over 18 years of age)

2EP5T

Ms/Mrs/Miss/Mr _____

Address _____

_____

_____ Postcode _____